About the author

After many years as a columnist and freelance writer, this is my first venture into the world of fiction and the book I always promised myself I would write. I am now retired, so cannot be accused of rushing into my literary career, and although most people might think I should be stepping away from the computer before dementia sets in, I have thoroughly enjoyed writing this story and hope readers will enjoy it as much as I have. When I'm not out walking or working my dogs, writing is my favourite go-to activity. Despite being a late starter, I am hoping to go on to add other titles to my portfolio, so perhaps the current lockdown situation due to the pandemic may well prove to be the best incentive.

BEASTS AND BUTTERFLIES

Wendy Beasley

BEASTS AND BUTTERFLIES

Vanguard Press

A CIP catalogue record for this title is
available from the British Library.

ISBN 978 1 784659 52 3

*Vanguard Press is an imprint of
Pegasus Elliot MacKenzie Publishers Ltd.*
www.pegasuspublishers.com

First Published in 2020

**Vanguard Press
Sheraton House Castle Park
Cambridge England**

Printed & Bound in Great Britain

Dedicated to Paul for his patience,
support and belief.

Prologue

Richard could feel the blood gushing from his neck as he tried to drag himself back through the open french windows across the floor towards the phone; but the effort was too much, and he collapsed onto the carpet, watching with horror as the crimson stain spread across the thick cream pile. He wasn't alone, but his visitor did nothing to assist him, and as the breeze drifted in from the open doors behind him, he drew it into his lungs in a last desperate attempt to stay alive. When he first saw the image of the stranger that had walked past him on the floor, and now stood watching him, he thought they'd come to save him; but he realised now that this wasn't the case! He tried to make some noise, to plead for help, but all that came out was a horrible gurgle, so he feebly raised his hand in a begging gesture. He could hear his own heartbeat and knew he must calm down or his life-blood would be pumped away before help arrived. But to his amazement, no help was summoned; instead, the person just sat down in the chair across the room, watching him, and then started to speak. For the first time in his whole life, Richard was afraid. Drifting in and out of consciousness, he heard most of what was said, and as he listened and began to make sense of the words, he realised with cold certainty that this person was never going to help him. In a desperate effort to reach the phone, he launched himself forward and was within touching distance when the speaker coldly and impassively stood up, walked forward, and moved it just out of his reach.

Chapter 1
THE END OF CHILDHOOD
1962

As I knocked on the big white door, as I'd done so many times before, I was trying to think what to say to my best friend Jessica Willcox, or Jess as I had always called her, because this time it was different. The door to this house was as familiar as my own, and most of my happiest childhood memories lay behind its formal exterior. However, all that changed when we were both thirteen, and as I waited for the door to open, I felt the sense of apprehension that had become so much a part of recent visits.

Jess and I had obviously had minor arguments over the years since we met at primary school, but never anything as bad as this, which had gone on for so long without apology or contact. It had been two weeks now since the big fall-out on the last day of the school term, and since then we had both stubbornly refused to see or speak to each other. It seemed so silly now, and I was struggling to remember how it became so serious, although I knew I'd been every bit as obstinate as she had. The last two weeks had been horrible. I'd been totally lost without her, and so I was really hoping that by now she felt the same. Since we first sat together as five-year-olds on our first day at school, we had been virtually inseparable, and after a horribly lonely two weeks, I was determined to try to sort things out, which is what brought me to this door. Once I had made up my mind, I had to do it straight away, before I lost my courage; but now I was here, I had no idea what I was going to say. Trying desperately to think of something that would sound friendly without seeming stupid, I realised my mistake when, much to my surprise, Jess's father Richard opened the door. When I'd decided to come, I was sure he would have gone to work, and I definitely wouldn't have made the visit if I'd known he was at home, as he was the reason for the argument in the first place. I was never quite sure about Richard, and had started to feel uncomfortable around him, so I stopped going round when he was there. Jess noticed this, and thought it was something she'd done to upset me, so kept asking what was wrong. I wasn't able to give her the reason as I didn't really understand it myself, and I could hardly say, "I'm not coming round because I don't like your Dad," so I made lame excuses, which she didn't believe and obviously thought I was lying, which upset her even more. Not knowing how to handle the situation, I'd become defensive, and it ended up in a blazing row where we both said things we didn't mean, which had brought us to this point.

Richard's smooth voice interrupted my thoughts. "Hello, Rachel, it's lovely to see you after such a long time. Do come in."

The feeling of uneasiness in the pit of my stomach put me on my guard. I just knew that I shouldn't go in, and I really wanted to turn and run. However, not knowing how to refuse, I decided to stick with Jess and avoid being alone with him; but when we reached the elegant drawing room with no sign of her, I started to feel anxious.

"I'm afraid you've missed Jess. I took her to the station this morning. She said she was fed up with being on her own, and wanted to spend the rest of the holidays with her cousins in Yorkshire. It seems that my company wasn't enough for her."

My heart sank; not only had I missed the chance of patching things up with Jess, but I had also let myself get into a situation I had been determined to avoid: alone in the house with Richard. I desperately tried to think of a way out, but unfortunately, not fast enough, and, almost immediately, he moved closer and tried to put his arm around me. My heart was racing and my mouth had gone dry, but gut instinct drove me, and I ducked around his arm and moved away, heading for the door. Trying desperately to think of something, anything to say that would make him leave me alone, all I came up with was, "I've got to go. I'm meant to be going to the shops for Mum, and she's waiting for the shopping."

He was unconvinced.

"Don't lie to me, Rachel. I know you really want to stay. Whatever you and Jess fell out about has kept you away too long, and I'm sure you've missed me as much as I have missed you. You're just a bit shy and embarrassed, but this is meant to happen; you're my special girl, and I'm just going to show you how much I love you. Come and give me a cuddle and I'll teach you how to make love."

Not waiting for any response, he crossed the room and grabbed me by the shoulders, turning me to face him. Although his voice was soft, his hands were rough, and as I struggled, his grip became harder and his breath came in short gasps. I twisted my face away as he tried to kiss me, but I could feel his hot breath as he fought with me, but still tried to convince me.

"You know I love you, Rachel, and I need you. Don't be afraid — this is what we both want."

I was terrified and started kicking out and screaming at him to let me go, as I tried to wriggle out of his vice-like grip; but then he hit me, and the shock left me reeling. My head felt as if it would explode from the blow and the tears ran down my face as his mood changed to anger and there was no more talk of love. His face was red and his breathing heavy, making my stomach heave at the sickly smell of his after-shave, which I knew I would never forget. I felt his spit in my face as he gasped out the words that really frightened me, and made me feel as if I had somehow done something bad and brought this on myself.

"Fucking little bitch, you've led me on for years, prancing around in front of me, sticking your tits out and parading your sexy little body; you knew what you were doing and I've done well to wait this long and let you grow up. Well, you're not a kid anymore and you know what you're doing, so stop cock teasing, and give me what I want. I'm going to give you the best fuck you are ever likely to get."

I couldn't understand what I had done to make him so angry, and yet some part of me wanted to say sorry, as if this would make everything right. Locking one arm around my neck so I could hardly breathe, he dragged me backwards into the room, and it was then I noticed the open French windows at the far end, and my survival instincts took over. If I could just break away and make it to the garden, I could run out of the back gate and home. I let myself go limp as if to give up and, as I had hoped, this allowed him to readjust his grip. Just as he did so, I used all my strength to wriggle out from under his arm and ran across the room, dodging round the settee in headlong flight. For a brief moment, I thought I had made it, but suddenly he was on me again, and with incredible determination he forced me down on the ground. Even as my face touched the thick cream carpet, I continued to fight, but I was losing the battle. I lay right beside the open French doors, but knew there was no hope of escape; and as Richard panted and tore at my clothes, I realised what was happening to me and yet, paralysed with fear, could do nothing to stop it. My own naive idea of what sex was all about in no way prepared me for the perverted onslaught that followed. The rape was brutal and painful; he seemed to get extra pleasure from slapping and biting me, growling like an animal and calling me vile names. It seemed to go on for ages, but was, in fact, over very quickly, as his frenzied attack brought him almost immediate release. I felt completely numb, and when I could no longer fight him, I tried very hard to pretend it wasn't happening, keeping my eyes focussed on the beautiful white rose bush outside the open French windows. The heady perfume of the flowers drifted in and filled my nostrils, and the creamy white blooms danced before my eyes through a mist of tears. When it was over, I was riveted with shock, and, sure that there would be some sort of apology, or sign of shame or regret, I turned my head to look at him — but there was no sign of pity or remorse.

As he caught me watching him, he dipped into his pocket and brought out a wallet. Peeling off a few notes from a substantial wad, he threw them down beside me and muttered something about getting myself a present; and then, almost as an afterthought, he said, "I'm not sure you earned all that. I think you can do a bit more for the money."

Undoing his zip, he pulled me up by my hair and thrust my face into his groin; but, after just a couple of suffocating seconds in the sticky, sweaty mess while he thrust himself into my face, he gave up and threw me back down on the floor.

"Get yourself dressed and out of my house," he said, as he did up his trousers and adjusted his belt. "I never want to see your face again, you dirty little slut. Take your money and go. Make no mistake, you got what you came for and I didn't come looking for you. You don't want to think you've got any sort of hold over me; it's all your fault, leading me on; you only got what you were asking for, and you loved it — didn't you — didn't you? I bet you're ready for some more."

Panic-stricken, I grabbed my clothes, carefully avoiding the money he'd flung on the floor, and got to my feet as I realised his voice was getting thicker and his breath was coming faster: he was actually getting excited again, and as his hand went back to his zip, I knew he was going to attack me again. I felt almost removed from my body, watching the crumpled and dishevelled girl desperately trying to dress; but I soon returned to reality when he made another grab for me and I dived out of his way, falling back down on the floor and once again at his mercy. Then, as if thinking better of it, he suddenly turned his back on me and was about to leave the room when he stopped, turned, and with a voice devoid of any emotion, he said, "If you tell anyone about this, they won't believe you; and even if they do, I will tell them you are nothing but a dirty little slut who teased me and led me on. So, you'd better keep your fucking mouth shut!"

Then he calmly walked out of the room and closed the door behind him.

Every fibre of my being told me to get up and run, and the breeze blowing in through the French windows reminded me that I still had a means of escape; but still my shocked body refused to move and I was racked with uncontrollable sobs. Then the fear kicked in. He might come back. I must get away, so I jumped to my feet and ran. Across the paved patio onto the lawn, and on through the beautiful garden, past the wicker chairs which I briefly thought might hide me, and on towards the side gate in the surrounding brick wall. I ran without seeing the stunning borders or the swinging hammocks where Jess and I had drunk lemonade and planned our futures just a short while ago. All the beauty and scents were lost on me in my headlong rush, and although the monster wasn't behind me, it felt as if he was.

I made it to the gate and, despite my terror that I would find it locked, it opened easily and I almost fell onto the pavement outside. I was sure I would find people and help as soon as I had escaped, but there wasn't a soul in sight; and so, not knowing what else to do, I continued to run, heading for home but without really wanting to arrive.

By the time I arrived at the door to my own house I had regained some sense of control and remembered the warnings; and, fearing he might do exactly as he said, I knew I couldn't say anything to my parents, which left no-one at all I could talk to.

Brushing the hair off my face and blowing my nose, I entered through the back door and went into the kitchen, where Mum sat engrossed in her knitting; and, with a non-committal greeting, I went straight up to my room. I knew as soon as I arrived in my bedroom that this was a bad idea as, with the bathroom downstairs, I had no way of cleaning myself up; and although I wouldn't be able to have a bath at this time of day without causing suspicion, I did need to wash and change my underwear.

I selected some clean things from my drawer and, hiding them under my jumper, went back downstairs and straight into the bathroom. Mum didn't seem to notice, and once inside I could strip off, wash, and hope that she wouldn't notice how long I was in there.

No amount of hot water and soap was enough, and although I washed and scrubbed as best I could in the limited time and space available, I didn't feel much cleaner when I finished and could still smell him on me. When I could wash no more, I came out of the bathroom and went back up to my room, leaving my underwear in the laundry basket; and when I closed my bedroom door I sat down on the bed, wondering what I should do next. I couldn't believe that so much could have happened to me without it showing, so I got up and looked in the mirror. My eyes were a bit puffy from crying, but this was starting to fade; and, other than a slight paleness, I looked the same as I had before my ordeal. My neck was a bit sore, but there was no visible sign of his grip on it and no bites and bruises were visible beneath my clothes, so although I couldn't escape the reminders, no-one else would see them. Satisfied that my secret was safe, and with an hour or so before lunch, I picked up a book from my shelf in the hope that reading would fill my mind — as it always did — and take me somewhere away from here. It was somewhat bizarre, in retrospect, that I chose a book about a teenager's crush on a boy in her class that I had been enjoying before, but it now held no interest for me and I didn't care whether she got with him or not, so I threw it down on the bed unopened. I felt I wanted to go out and walk and just keep walking to nowhere in particular, but I was afraid to go out in case I encountered him again; and then I started worrying about what I would say to Jess and whether I could ever face her or anyone else again.

Sleep is a wonderful healer, and as I lay on my bed, not knowing what to do or how to act, my shocked body came to my rescue and I drifted off into a deep and peaceful sleep.

It was lunchtime before my Mum's strident voice awoke me from my slumber.

"Rachel, whatever are you doing up there? Come down now — it's lunchtime and your Dad's waiting."

I jumped off the bed, feeling guilty for some unknown reason, and then, remembering the morning's events, I looked once again in the mirror before going down. My face had returned to normal; no puffiness or terror was visible, and so I headed downstairs to begin the charade that was now my life.

Chapter 2
REFLECTIONS
1979

When I emerged into the sunshine from the gloom of the solicitor's office, I was in a state of shock. The bright sunlight did nothing to lift the feeling of melancholy and dread which had descended on me as I had listened to the coldly superior lawyer just a few moments ago. Sitting in his dusty book-lined office, and with a voice lacking any emotion or even feigned interest, he told me my mother had died and left me the cottage, which had been my childhood home. I felt the room closing in on me and knew I must get out; so, mumbling about needing some air and promising to come back in a moment, I almost ran from the office past a startled receptionist and out onto the street. I stood on the pavement with traffic streaming past me and fought to regain some composure and get my breath. With my back to the low wall surrounding the office I had just vacated, and my hands either side of me gripping on to it for support, the feelings of panic gradually subsided. I knew I must look very strange to passers-by, but didn't feel able to go back in yet; and, much as I wanted to, I couldn't really just go home. I needed time to think, and although not religious, the churchyard on the other side of the road looked deserted and inviting, so I waited for a break in the traffic and headed across. The old wooden gate hung open invitingly, although on closer inspection it was obvious that it could neither close nor open any wider than its present stationary position, having parted company with its upper hinge and sunk its corner resolutely into the soft earth in an effort to keep upright. Once through the gate and walking up the gravel path, I had no idea where I was heading, but then I noticed the Memorial benches placed against the church walls for those needing tranquil contemplation. I felt justified in using one for just such a purpose, although I wasn't sure my contemplation would be anything like tranquil. As I approached one of the benches situated at the front of the beautiful old church, the soft sunlight peeking through the leaves on the surrounding trees danced on the brass plaque on the backrest, commemorating a long-dead parishioner, and I felt a brief moment of envy for his peace. As I sat down on the bench made warm by the sunlight, I felt the tension leave my body and realised I had been pushing my nails into the palms of my hands. I took a deep breath and made myself exhale slowly in an effort to calm my troubled thoughts and make sense of them. I wished I could just sit and forget the events of the past hour, but as the church clock chimed the present time, I allowed my mind to drift back into the past. Suddenly, I was thirteen again, back in the kitchen of the cottage, facing my father's fury as he ranted and raved, while my mother wept and wailed about the disgrace I had brought to the family.

This was the most emotion I had seen from either of my parents in my entire life, and looking back I found it amazing that they were capable of such deep feeling, albeit for the most part anger and shame, with absolutely no hint of love. Neither of my parents had ever been great talkers and, strange as it now seemed, I had accepted their reticence and never questioned it or them. I had picked up a bit about their background from snippets of overheard conversation and some of my Grandad's casual comments, but never from them. However, I was a curious child and went out of my way to encourage Grandad to talk; and, over the years, as I watched him toil in the garden, I learned that my father, George Sutton, was a Norfolk boy born and bred. After growing up in a tithe cottage as the son of a farm labourer, it was both natural and expected that he would leave school at fourteen and go to work on the same farm as his father. When George reached twenty, his father had retired and he'd taken over most of the work and had proved himself indispensable to the ageing farmer. At about that time, a chance trip to Ipswich to watch his beloved Norwich City Football Club play brought him into contact with eighteen-year-old Essex born Alice. She and her brother Donald had gone to watch the game and they met George in the queue for tickets and got talking. Even though technically they were on different sides, George hit it off with both Alice and her brother Donald, and arranged to go for a drink with them after the match; and this was the beginning of his frequent trips to Essex, where it became apparent that he was far more interested in Alice than Donald. This was quite an adventurous thing for a village boy to do, as it was far more usual for country boys to find a wife in their own village, so George must have been keen. It certainly came as a bit of a shock to me when I heard it, as I couldn't imagine my Dad being keen on anything, and certainly not in any way romantic; and even now, in the midst of all my other dark memories, this thought brought a slight smile to my lips.

It was obvious from the next piece of the story, which came from Grandad, that he was very proud of how well his son, my Dad, had done. He told me that when the farmer realised why Dad was going away every weekend, and saw that he was serious about this girl, he offered him the old derelict cottage on a part-rent/part-buy deal if he would do the work to make it habitable. Dad apparently snatched at this opportunity, for it was very unusual for someone in his position to be able to buy a house; and over the next couple of years, in between working and visiting Alice, he set about turning the cottage into a home. Although he didn't have much in the way of design skills, he did manage to make it warm, watertight and structurally sound, and he ensured that they had an indoor toilet and a bathroom, which was by no means common in country cottages at that time. He certainly worked hard both on the cottage and at work, and his hard labour and overtime money meant that by the time he and Alice married, he had a home to bring her to, and had almost managed to pay it off.

I learned the rest much later from my Grandmother, who seemed to have a greater awareness of what her daughter thought and felt, and some understanding of how she later treated me.

When they had first married, they were reasonably happy, and Alice enjoyed looking after George and the cottage, which kept her busy. George's father often came round and helped her in the garden, and before long, she had a pretty garden with a very useful vegetable patch. When she found out she was pregnant, she was happy, although a little scared, but nothing prepared her for the long and difficult ordeal of the birth, and although she loved baby Thomas Michael with a passion that surprised her, she made up her mind that she would never go through it again. The loss of the baby at just a few months old from cot death left them both devastated, but rather than bringing them together, it drove them apart, with each one questioning the other as to the possible cause of his tragic death. Alice and George Sutton were not blessed with much imagination, and the only strong love either of them had ever felt was for the child that had been snatched away. When the baby died, George just worked longer and longer hours on the farm, and Alice, possibly still suffering from post-natal depression, sank further and further into melancholy, until, driven by desperation, she went to see her doctor.

It was this kindly doctor, recognising Alice's depression and the cause of it, who suggested they might try for another baby; but, faced with Alice's almost hysterical refusal to go through it all again, he broached the subject of adoption. Although she initially said no, after thinking about it for a few days she realised that this might be the best way to give George the family he wanted without the pain; so, taking the doctor's suggestion on board, she brought the subject up with George, and surprisingly he seemed to think it was a good idea. Initially, they were determined to have a boy, but the adoption society said that if they wanted a young child, they would do better not to specify gender as they may have to wait a long time; but if they had a girl now, they could always try for a boy later. Alice wasn't sure how she felt about two children, but George seemed very keen on the idea, so they took the advice and accepted me. Unfortunately, although just a baby in need of love, I in no way made up for the wonderful Thomas, and Alice found it very hard to bond with me. Everything about me seemed alien, and she kept wondering what my real family was like. She became obsessed about my background, and for some reason she was convinced that my family were bad people, and that I would turn out bad just like them. She told George of her fears; but rather than putting her mind at rest, he agreed that she did have a point, and they would have to keep an eye on me to see if I developed any undesirable tendencies.

All these years later, as I let my mind revisit the past, I feel so sad for the innocent baby that had been me, and had never had a real chance of love. I could see again the dark, dingy kitchen with the stone floor and tiny windows that ensured the room was always in semi-darkness, and the heavy curtains that virtually obscured the small panes of glass and further reduced the little light that filtered in. On that particular day, the kitchen light was on as always, but it did nothing to lift the dark cloud that had descended on the family. I sat at the table with my head bowed, and nervously picked at the cloth that covered it, feeling hurt and confused and, for the first time in my life, fearful of the man who was bellowing at me. I could sense the look of disappointment on my mother's face, even though she stood behind me; but if I was honest with myself, I had to admit that she usually wore that look whenever her eyes fell on me, almost as if nothing I ever did could match up to her expectations.

"You're a disgrace, and I can hardly bear to look at you," she said between sobs, which really upset me. But my father's rage was far more frightening. He was short but thickset and, as he bent over me huddled on the kitchen chair, he seemed every bit as intimidating as Richard had been a few short weeks ago. His words cut into me like a knife, and I can still remember the nausea and dizziness that swept over me as he, like Richard before him, hurled abuse at me.

"You're nothing but a dirty slut, carrying on with boys at your age. You are no daughter of ours! It's bad blood, that's what it is, nothing to do with us!"

There it was, that word again, and although I barely understood it when Richard had spat it at me, here it was again from my own father. What was it that I wasn't aware of but they could see? Was I truly as bad as everyone seemed to be telling me? If so, I had no idea what to do or how to make it better. I remembered putting my head down on the heavy chenille tablecloth covering the old oak table, while the tears that fell from my eyes formed a large dark pool on the cloth. Dad kept shouting at me, demanding to know who the father was, but I was so scared of what would happen if I told him, that I kept my mouth shut, even though I was terrified and felt so dreadfully alone.

Looking back now at the time before the attack, I realise I had been a lively, outgoing and confident child growing up in the liberal sixties, where everything seemed new and exciting, even in our small village. Although I was surprised to discover that my rather weary, reticent parents had adopted me after the death of their infant son, it didn't particularly worry me. I could find no similarity between myself and the picture of baby Thomas Michael on the sideboard, who was always discussed in hushed and reverent tones, and I was certainly nothing like my parents. When I was around six, I asked Mum about this, and she didn't attempt to hide the fact of my adoption. There was no doubt in my mind I was destined to be a "replacement" for their angelic offspring; but, even at that young age, I was aware that I hadn't met the criteria. Much later, I discovered that baby Thomas only lived a few short months, and so had no time to be anything but perfect, and I was painfully aware that I had no chance of replacing this angelic figure, no matter what I did. I do remember wondering if I, too, had been perfect to my own real mother, and to make myself feel better I invented stories about her, and her reasons for giving me up. They all involved tragedy, as for me that was the only explanation that I could face. To begin with I did ask questions, but was never told anything about my real family, and it was made clear that my questions were unwelcome, so I stopped asking. At the time, I wasn't particularly worried about this, as it allowed me to invent my own fantasies, which kept me happy for several years. However, later on, when I began to develop my own personality, I became much more curious about my background. My parents were at a loss to understand the bubbly extrovert daughter they had raised, but although undemonstrative and unable to show love, they were not unkind to me, and I had never before known real anger. So this terrible outburst came as a complete shock, especially the cruel things my father said about my real family, and I started to believe that maybe he was right and whatever I did and no matter how hard I tried I was just no good; that is what Richard had said, and now here was Dad saying it, too.

Looking back now, although I had never stopped feeling guilty, I realised that it wasn't my fault. At twelve years old, when the abuse had begun, my knowledge of the facts of life was limited to some giggly comments from older but not necessarily wiser friends, and I just thought Jess's father was playing. Neither Jess nor I had siblings, and we found in each other the sister we both needed. My parents didn't like people coming to the house, so I often went to Jess's after school, and her mum Helen always seemed pleased to see me. She was very kind and always seemed to be smiling, and to me, with her thick, wild sandy hair tied back in a loose ponytail and freckles all over her face, she looked like everything a mother should be — I adored her. She always took an interest in everything we had been doing throughout the day, served up a lovely tea and joined in with all the messy painting and gluing sessions on the kitchen table. Although she was often part of our games or even the instigator, as we got older, she was also happy to let us be ourselves, and never interfered or asked questions when we were giggling over some pop star or talking in excited whispers about a boy we both liked. Jess's house was huge in comparison to mine, an imposing Georgian manor house at the end of the village, with a large walled garden and sweet-scented magnolia blossoms draped over the copings. It seemed like a palace to me, and on summer days when we were little we would play in the garden, pretending we were princesses or fairy queens. I loved the wicker chairs that stood around like hooded monks, allowing the sitter to be completely hidden, and the hammocks strung between the trees, which bore witness to our most private conversations. When we got older, we would just lie on the grass, topping up our suntans and dreaming of our future, which we had no doubt would be wonderful.

All this ended when tragedy struck, and Helen died in a car accident. At just twelve years old, I had no way of knowing how to deal with this, and although I really wanted to go to Jess, my Mum said I should keep away as it was a private time of family loss and I wouldn't be welcome. So I stopped my visits and left Jess to deal with her grief without me, and when I did see her again a few weeks later, I had no idea what to do or say to help, so for a while our friendship faltered.

When she came back to school after an absence of several weeks, she came looking for me, and although she was quieter than usual, as far as I could tell she seemed to be coping. She didn't want to talk about her Mum, but this suited me, as I could think of nothing helpful to say, so we just picked up where we left off. I did notice a new moodiness with other people — she seemed a bit reticent and withdrawn with anyone else — but I just presumed that was a normal part of grief and she was always okay with me.

"Good afternoon."

This polite greeting from a passing stranger made me jump and dragged me back from my memories. I nodded and smiled at the friendly old chap, as I struggled to remember where I was and get a grip on reality. Once he'd gone, I closed my eyes again and rested back on the bench, feeling the warm sunshine on my face and listening to the birds singing in the churchyard trees.

It all started quite suddenly. Jess's Dad Richard was at home more since her Mum had died, and although I realised he must be upset, too, he didn't seem to show it; but I thought he was putting on a brave face to try to help Jess cope with the loss of her mother. I hadn't seen much of him before, and on the few times he'd been at home he seemed rather remote and unfriendly. Though not very tall, he was quite heavy, while his silver-grey hair and horn-rimmed glasses gave him a superior air, and I had always been a little afraid of him. However, since the accident he'd changed and seemed much more fun, organising games just as Jess's Mum had done. Richard's games were much rowdier than we had played before, and Hide and Seek or Squeak Piggy Squeak always ended with kisses for forfeits and lots of cuddles and giggles. Although it seemed a little odd and even disloyal to be playing and laughing with Richard so soon after Helen's death, I did quite enjoy it in the beginning. With such undemonstrative parents, I was unused to physical contact, and yet really wanted to feel loved, and I thought Richard was wonderful. I even wished my own father was more like him; but that soon began to change when his kisses became more frequent and the cuddles took on an intimacy that made me feel uncomfortable. Sometimes, when he caught me in a game of chase or hide and seek, he seemed reluctant to let me go, and I began to feel really uneasy and embarrassed.

I did notice that Jess avoided these games and always seemed to make an excuse not to play, and at first, I thought that this was because she was missing her Mum, and felt guilty about having fun; but she looked more frightened than guilty, so I didn't understand what was troubling her. As time went by, the games became progressively rougher and I often found myself gripped and manhandled in a way that didn't feel right. Richard would find excuses to send Jess out of the room to make drinks or fetch something, and as soon as she left the room, he would ask me to sit next to him and give him a hug, saying how lonely he was since his wife died. Then he started asking me personal questions, and always seemed breathless when wanting to know whether I had a boyfriend or had started wearing a bra or make-up, and I thought that his behaviour was very odd. I avoided being alone with him, and started making excuses not to visit the house, but that upset Jess, who wanted to know what was the matter, and I made excuses about needing to be at home, which she clearly didn't believe. We finally had the big row about me not coming round at the end of the Summer Term when we were both thirteen, and I remembered her telling me not to bother coming round ever again and storming off.

At first, I thought this was for the best, and at least I didn't need to think of any more excuses; but after a couple of weeks on my own, I realised how much I missed her, and knew I had to go and see her, even if it meant putting up with Richard.

It was a hot afternoon when I finally summoned up the courage and headed for Jess's house. I kept going over in my mind what I would say when I got there. I knew Richard worked from home most of the time, but I had seen his car heading out of the village that morning and so had decided that this would be the day to make up with Jess.

"Are you all right?" Once again, a concerned voice brought me back to the present time, and I realised with some embarrassment why the woman was staring at me — tears were running down my face, and I brushed them away with my hand.

"Yes, thanks, I'm fine, just a bit of hay fever." I tried to sound convincing.

That was the last time I had seen Richard, but as I closed my eyes and leaned back on the wooden bench almost seventeen years later, I could still see his smirking face, feel his hot breath and smell that sickly aftershave, and I felt myself shiver in spite of the warmth from the sun.

Chapter 3
GROWING UP

Looking back now, I could see how that day had changed me from a confident, bubbly extrovert to a morose teenager, as quiet and reticent as the parents that raised me.

It was a month or so after the attack that I started to feel sick, and from the little bit of sex education I had at school, I began to understand what was happening to me, and realised with horror that I was pregnant. I had no idea what to do and was terrified of what my parents would say, so decided to do nothing. In a desperate effort to play for time while I tried to work out what to do, I started wearing baggy jumpers and pretended to have an upset tummy, but my mother's searching looks gave way to suspicions, and she insisted on taking me to the doctor. She stayed in the room throughout the examination, and although I knew what the doctor would say, I was praying he wouldn't say it. It seems it came as no surprise to my mother either, but from the moment that the doctor confirmed the pregnancy, she treated me with utter contempt. The sexual revolution of the swinging sixties brought about by the revolutionary contraceptive pill hadn't yet reached our small Norfolk village, and an unmarried mother was still a disgrace, with abortions neither contemplated nor available. Once my father heard of my predicament, he too, could hardly bear to look at me, and both he and my mother were ashamed, disgusted and angry. It never occurred to them that I had been anything but a willing party, and it seemed they had an overriding need to find out who was responsible. With Richard's warnings still ringing in my ears, I couldn't tell them what had happened, but they saw this as defiance and wilfulness, and over the following months the scene replayed repeatedly, and the pressure became more intense. If only they knew how much I needed to tell someone what had happened to me. Had they been softer and more patient with me I may have weakened, but they just kept up their accusations and became more and more angry, until finally they admitted defeat and packed me off to my adoptive grandmother in Essex to hide my shame from the village.

My grandmother, Janet Wilson, was a far kinder, warmer person than my mother and it was difficult to believe they were mother and daughter. Nan had always taken an interest in me and brought me things whenever she visited. She would play games with me, and she took time teaching me to knit and crochet and, better still, she would give me hugs and kisses when I was small, which my mother never did. Nan had always lived in a modest three-bedroomed house on a housing estate a couple of miles outside the county town of

Chelmsford, and we had visited her there a couple of times when I was a toddler. I hadn't been there for years, but thought this was where I was going to live, as no-one had bothered to tell me she'd moved. Later, she told me how she and her husband, who I had never met, had moved to the house when it was new, and both her son and daughter had been born there. My mother had grown up in that house and it was from there that she left for her wedding to George Sutton. Nan and her husband were pleased with the match and very impressed that their daughter was going to go and live in a newly modernised cottage that George had bought and paid for. However, Nan was sad to see her go so far away, and when her son Donald got a job in London and her husband died soon after, she found herself all alone with very few visitors. She decided to sell the house that was full of memories and make a new start in a small two-bedroomed flat on the other side of town, and it was to here that I was despatched in my disgrace. Despite the unconventional circumstances, after being so lonely I think she was quite pleased to provide me with a temporary home. Doubtless she was both shocked and a little disappointed at my condition, but she didn't let it stand in the way of her kindness, and she did her very best to support me and prepare me for what was to come.

Even though there was no discussion in my hearing and no-one ever consulted me, I came to understand that the baby would be adopted. This didn't bother me as I just wanted rid of it, and as the birth drew nearer, Nan arranged visits from social workers to discuss things with me, hoping I would show some sort of interest.

I had no wish to talk to them and I just sat and listened as they talked at me. There was no attempt at counselling, and no-one seemed to care what happened to me, and I soon realised that the only person of any importance in this whole situation was the child. Like my parents before them, they assumed I had got myself into this whole sorry mess and, as if to confirm their opinion of me, I had an overwhelming feeling of guilt, as well as disgust at myself, my bulging body and the thing that was growing inside me. Although Nan tried to be kind and understanding, she really had no idea what was going on in my head, and when I refused to discuss the baby, she became a little exasperated and I could feel her losing patience with me. I so wanted to talk to someone, to explain what had really happened to me, and find out what I should do next, but I feared what would happen if I did. I was only just fourteen years old and had no idea how to handle the situation in which I found myself. Separated from everything familiar, and too terrified to tell anyone the truth, I drifted through the pregnancy in a sort of guilt-ridden haze, unwilling or unable to consider the future for the baby or myself.

When the pain started, I almost welcomed it, and a small part of me hoped it would kill me, and then I wouldn't have to deal with what would come next. However, as the pain became more intense, I became very frightened and, surrounded by strangers, with no-one to hold my hand or encourage me, I felt totally abandoned. Although I had no way of knowing, the birth was relatively easy with no complications, and in quite a short while I heard the first cry and then silence. The atmosphere in the room suddenly changed and I stopped being the focus of attention as the medical staff gathered round the child on the end of the bed, and then one of them swooped it up in a blanket and rushed off to the other side of the room. I could barely see what was happening, and so I asked one of the nurses what was wrong.

"He's just a bit poorly, love; we need to get him breathing properly."

"He," I thought — so he was a little boy, and he was poorly. It was probably because I didn't want him, and so now, as a punishment, he was going to die, and it wasn't his fault; he didn't ask to be born. I had to do something, tell him to breathe, tell him to live, but as I sat up and tried to get off the bed, a wave of dizziness and nausea swept over me and I fell back onto the pillows. At that moment, I heard him cry and keep on crying, and relief overwhelmed me. That was it, he was my son, and when he was put in my arms the power of my love for him was instant and overwhelming. Gone were all thoughts of Richard, and here was perfection — an amazing tiny bundle with eyes fixed on my face and a helpless vulnerability that was irresistible. The bond between us was forged and I felt some of my old fire return. I knew I was ready to fight to keep my son, the only real family I had. When I told Nan my decision, she agreed to speak to my parents to ask them if I could bring him home; but, far from making me welcome, they completely disowned me. I had one conversation with my mother on the phone when she made it clear that I wasn't to return to the village with my bastard son, and if I insisted on keeping him then I could consider myself on my own. Nan was more sympathetic, partly, I think, because she, too, had fallen victim to the baby's charm, and over the next few years she helped me take care of him.

Although I wanted nothing more to do with my parents, and had already started using Nan's name Wilson instead of my own, I named my son Thomas Michael after my dead adoptive brother. I have no idea why I chose these names, unless perhaps in a pathetic effort to curry favour or just down to a lack of imagination; but for whatever reason, he was never really a Thomas and so was always known as Tom.

The overwhelming love I felt for Tom took me by complete surprise, and the fear of losing him consumed me. I could hardly let him out of my sight, and was reluctant to let anyone else near him. I am sure Nan felt quite hurt as I refused her offers of help, but the bit of me that still felt guilty saw Tom, much as I loved him, as my penance. Fortunately, Tom was a very easy, contented baby, and gradually I began to relax and allow Nan back into our lives. I would never have managed without her help, and as soon as I accepted this, things settled down into a routine and the years slid by.

Chapter 4
LIFE GOES ON

Once Tom started nursery and Nan could take and pick him up, I managed to start work and contribute to the household, which made me feel much better and definitely eased the financial burden for Nan. I was lucky enough to get the office junior position advertised at our local bank, and although to begin with it was just filing, photocopying and making tea, I really enjoyed it. The girls I worked with were friendly and helpful and the manager was kind and patient and took a fatherly interest in me, and gradually allowed me to do a bit more. Over the years, staff came and left, with all the usual invitations to parties, weddings and christenings, and I really enjoyed the social side as well as the work. I eventually worked my way up to Chief Cashier and, much as I loved Nan and enjoyed living with her, I felt it was time to find my own place. I knew it was getting more difficult for her as she got older, and the flat was a bit too small for us all now Tom was growing up. The prospect of moving out was quite terrifying, but I was becoming concerned about Tom growing up in an all-female household and hoped that with my own house I would have more chance of inviting friends and couples round, and thus give Tom at least some part-time male role models. I had a nice circle of friends, some of which were men, but there was no special man in my life, nor could there be, since I could never face the thought of any sort of physical intimacy. Despite this, there was no shortage of friends' husbands willing to take Tom to the odd football game or for a couple of hours fishing with their own kids, so I didn't think he was missing out too much, although I found out later on that things were not quite as easy for Tom as I thought. In the early days he didn't really miss having a father as he'd no idea he should have one. He knew he was loved and his world was safe and warm, so it didn't seem in any way unusual that there were two women and no men in his life. However, he told me much later that all this changed when he went to school, although he never talked to me about it at the time, and I had no idea things were so difficult for him. He said that it was then that the questions started — Where was his Daddy? Why didn't he have a Daddy? Which one was his Mummy?

Children can be very cruel, and when he didn't have any answers, the kids started making up their own, telling him that his father had taken one look at him and run away, and that I was really his sister as I wasn't old enough to be his mother. They even told him that Nan and I had stolen him from his real parents.

Unbeknown to me, this had a very bad effect on him and he went from a smiling, confident boy to a sullen and uncommunicative teenager. Apparently, it seemed to him that with a lack of any other reasonable explanation his tormentors might be right, but in my ignorance I thought it was just a teenage thing and would pass.

Oblivious to his suffering, I went ahead with my plans to move, not realising that this would just unsettle him further. I managed to find a nice little flat to rent not too far from Nan, but it was in a different catchment area, and for a while, things did seem better. Tom didn't see much of his old school friends now and had found some new ones, and although I hadn't met them, he seemed much happier; but neither of us were prepared for the shock of the sudden death of Nan. I had thought perhaps she was missing us, as she didn't seem to go out as much lately and appeared more tired than usual, so I tried to visit as often as possible, and I know Tom went round two or three times a week, but she just didn't seem to be herself. However, I wasn't overly concerned about it and so was in no way ready for the phone call at work to say she was in hospital, in intensive care following a severe heart attack. I rushed off to see her and just managed to get to the hospital before she died, and was able to tell her how much she meant to me, even though I am not sure if she heard. In my haste to get to her side, I hadn't managed to get in touch with Tom, and by the time I did manage to contact him it was too late, so he was never able to say his goodbyes. I know he blamed me for this, and I really wished I had been able to take him with me, but if I had delayed, she wouldn't have seen either of us before she died.

Nan had been such an important part of both of our lives, and losing her put a terrible strain on our relationship, as we both struggled to deal with our grief. Until the last few weeks, I had never known her to be anything but hale and hearty, and so couldn't believe she'd gone. Although now completely grown up and in charge of my own life, I had always known that Nan was there for me, and losing her left me feeling almost as alone and frightened as I had been all those years ago. Tom was now all the family I had, and I had this confirmed a few years previously, when Nan had told me Dad had died. Even though she asked Mum to see me, she refused, and wouldn't even allow me to go to the funeral. This wasn't really a surprise, as in all the years since Tom's birth they had never once enquired about either me or him.

Within days of Nan's death, Uncle Donald had appeared on the scene and taken charge of all the formalities, leaving me nothing to do but grieve. Although I knew it was Donald's right to sort out his mother's things, I didn't know him well, and had seen very little of him when she was alive, so couldn't help feeling that he was perhaps invading the privacy of the woman that was almost a mother to me. I found it extraordinary that ever since I had come to live with Nan my own mother had never come to see us, and even if she didn't want to see me, I thought she would have wanted to see her own mother. It seemed that although they sent me to live with her, they expected her to persuade me to give up the baby, and when she failed to do this, they had no more to do with her. When Donald arrived to sort everything out, I was sure she would come as well, but she neither came to help nor to the funeral, so even though I knew she was on her own since my Dad died, it would seem that being alone was better than being with me and the grandson she'd never seen.

I really missed Nan, and as the weeks went by after her death, her loss remained like a nagging pain. I hadn't realised how much I valued the visits, which I had convinced myself were for her benefit, and yet without the regular chats where we put the world to rights and talked about Tom and what was best for him, I felt cast out and alone. The enormity of facing the future and dealing with Tom without her back-up and reassurance was really daunting, and I was so busy worrying about this that I didn't see how badly her death had affected him, until the police called to say that they had arrested him! He and a couple of friends had vandalised a bus shelter, and I was horrified to learn that he'd assaulted a police officer.

I was sure there was some sort of mistake; even though he'd become difficult lately, he'd never shown any sign of violence. I realised he was struggling to cope with losing Nan, and for some reason he seemed to blame me; but this latest revelation just proved how far apart we had become, and how little I knew him anymore. We had been in disagreement even before Nan died about his wish to leave school after his exams, while I thought sixteen was too young and he should stay on for A levels, so we were not exactly seeing eye to eye. I was hoping that Nan would be able to talk some sense into him, but now she'd gone, and I had to get through to a boy who clearly resented me and preferred to spend his time with people I didn't even know. Now he was in trouble and I had no idea what to do to help him, or who to turn to. On the few previous times that Donald had visited Nan, he'd shown no interest in either Tom or me, and so I didn't feel I could ask him for help. However, I really needed some advice on how to handle this situation, as Tom's behaviour was totally out of character, and I was at a loss to know what to do for the best. In spite of his present predicament, I couldn't believe that he'd suddenly turned into a bad lot, and was inclined to think it was more about the company he was keeping. He'd become friendly with a different crowd since the start of the school holidays, and although I had never met any of them, these new friends seemed to be turning Tom into a sullen and rebellious boy with little time or respect for his mother or anyone else.

With no-one to call on, I had to go to the police station on my own and wait for Tom. Fortunately, after interviewing him for some time, they decided on a formal caution rather than a court case. They delivered a firm talking to, and a warning that a second offence would automatically result in charges, and then they allowed him to come home. Even though he seemed chastened by the experience, I wasn't convinced that he was reformed, and was fearful of him getting into more trouble. It was with this worry heavy on my mind, and just a few weeks after losing Nan, that I heard from the solicitor that my mother had also died, and I was the sole beneficiary of her possessions, which included the tiny cottage in the Norfolk village where I had grown up so suddenly and prematurely. Even though there was no will, paperwork in the house revealed that there was a daughter, and the solicitors set about finding me. It had taken some time to track me down because of the name change, so it seemed my mother had, in fact, died before Nan, so that would explain why she had not been at the funeral. It seemed that she'd not only kept her mother at a distance, but had also lost contact with her brother, so none of her family knew of her death. When I was finally located, all the formalities were complete, and it was just a case of taking possession, which is why I was at the solicitor's office that afternoon.

When I heard the news, my first instinct was to run. I didn't want the cottage or anything from it, and the thought of going back to the village, even briefly, to dispose of her legacy filled me with panic. I really missed Nan and wanted her advice; I knew that she would have understood how I felt, and been able to tell me what to do for the best. Even though it made no sense at all, the realisation that both my parents were dead left me feeling a strange sense of loss, and I found myself remembering my young life, before the events that had driven me away. Remembering the cottage brought me no comfort, as ever since my desperate run away from my attacker, which had brought me to the back-door gasping for breath, it held only bad memories of anger, bewilderment and fear. I could think of nothing worse than going back, and made an instant decision to just sell it and benefit from the cash; but then, unbidden, a new thought entered my head — a new start for Tom!

The more I tried to reject the idea, the more it made sense. Tom had nothing to fear from the village; no-one would know him there. He could get a job, if that was what he wanted, and after so many years, with the change of name, it was unlikely that anyone would remember me. Even if Richard was still in the village, I felt sure he would have forgotten all about me, and I realised that with maturity had come an impenetrable shell which I was determined would safeguard me against him and my memories. Even with Nan's help, it hadn't been easy bringing Tom up alone, juggling work with child-minding and struggling to keep a roof over our heads. Here at last was an opportunity to own property, albeit just a tiny cottage, and, with no rent or mortgage to pay, I could afford to take the voluntary redundancy which the bank was offering in its latest streamlining drive. I would still have to work, of course, but perhaps just a part-time job would bring in enough and leave me time to concentrate on my long-held ambition to write for a living; something that I knew I was good at, but had sadly neglected since leaving school. Perhaps now, in death, my parents could give us the security and happiness they had denied us in life.

After wiping my eyes, taking a deep breath and with a new sense of purpose, I stood up and headed back into the solicitor's office, much to the surprise of both him and his receptionist, who clearly thought that the mad woman was not coming back. Once the paperwork was complete, and signatures obtained, I set off for home. I had made my decision, and there was no going back; and, almost immediately, I felt better. Sitting on the top deck of the bus on the way home, the planning began. The one thing I was sure of was that I didn't want to go back as Ellie Sutton, and needed to work on a completely new identity. Because of this, we wouldn't be able to move straight into the cottage or the villagers would soon put two and two together, and realise who I was. It was important that Tom finished his exams, and it would take time for me to apply for and get my redundancy sorted out. I also realised with a start that Tom didn't yet know and had to agree; making all these plans without him even knowing was destined for disaster and, for a moment, I felt all my resolve leaving me. However, I brushed this aside, took another deep breath and continued planning. I suddenly had a bright idea. Julie, my friend at the bank, was married to an estate agent, and I hoped he may do me a favour by putting up a For Sale board for a few weeks and then replace it with one saying it was sold. I may have to be a bit inventive with the reason for this, but I felt sure this would convince the villagers that I had sold the property without ever returning. I didn't want to lie to my friends, but I couldn't see any other way round it, and I wasn't hurting anyone. Once I moved, I probably wouldn't ever see them again, and I convinced myself that if they knew my reasons they would understand.

The more I thought about the idea the more excited I became, and I felt sure I could pull it off. I had completely changed my appearance just after Tom was born. I was tired of the waist-length dark mane of hair which had always been my most distinguishing feature, but had been neglected and become dull, so I had it cut into a smart bob and had kept it short ever since. When I was looking for work and wanting to look more grown-up, I started wearing make-up and added some colour to my hair. The rich auburn tint added to the final rinse gave it a coppery glow, and together with the added maturity of the intervening years and childbirth, I looked completely different from the child that had left the village.

I saw her in my mind now, a pathetic, frightened child with head lowered so that the hair covered most of her face, feeling nothing but shame, and I realised how far I had come since then. My parents wouldn't allow me to register Tom in their name, and so I took my grandmother's name of Wilson and reverted to Rachel rather than the shortened form of Ellie that I had begun using when I was small. I didn't think that Rachel

Wilson arriving in the village with her son would ring any bells, and I could use the story I had invented many years ago of the young widow, whose husband had been killed when their son was an infant. I blamed a car accident and stole the details from what I could remember of the death of Jess's mother, and the curious soon stopped asking questions. Although I felt guilty about the deception, it had been easier to stick to this story with Tom rather than tell him the truth about his father, and he seemed to accept it. Despite the nagging voice in the back of my head that told me he had a right to know the truth, I decided to continue with it, in the hope that he would never need to know, and the villagers would have no cause for gossip.

Now all that remained was to convince Tom that this move would be in his best interests, and surprisingly, this proved much easier than anticipated.

Tom was already home when I got back from the solicitor's and, thinking there was no time like the present, I launched into my pitch, fully expecting strong opposition.

"Tom, how would you like to move?"

"What?" He lifted his head from a gardening catalogue, and not for the first time I was conscious of his dark good looks, and so glad he bore no resemblance to his father. He had my dark colouring but was tall and lean, unlike Richard's bulk or my slight frame, and I could only imagine that some of my "real" family must have had an influence on my son's make-up.

"I asked if you would like to move," I repeated. "Only I had the chance to buy a really cheap cottage in Norfolk, and it seemed too good an opportunity to miss... So, I — er, went ahead and bought it, and, well, I would really like us to move in."

It all came out in a bit of a rush and I realised how absurd it was that I was nervous of my own son and desperate for his approval. It didn't help that he was gazing at me with his mouth open, as if I had taken leave of my senses; but, determined to press on and not be deterred by his reaction, I had a sudden flash of inspiration, prompted by the magazine in his lap.

"I know it would have been better to talk about it first, but I had to make up my mind very quickly or I would have lost it, and if you really don't want to move I will just rent it out and keep it as an investment; but..." — time for my master shot — "it does have a lovely garden!"

He definitely took that piece of information on board, but remained unconvinced. "I don't know anything about Norfolk, and all my friends are here; why would I want to move?"

I detected a degree of panic in his voice, but I was ready for this argument.

"I don't think your friends have done much for you lately except get you into a lot of trouble, and now Nan has gone I thought you might like to get away from here, make a new start and perhaps some new friends."

As soon as the words were out of my mouth, I regretted criticising his friends, sure that he would leap to their defence — but I was wrong. It had obviously touched a raw nerve and for the first time in ages, he seemed to want to talk.

"They don't want me around anymore anyway," he said sullenly. "I am apparently a liability."

"What do they mean by that?" I asked.

"They think that the police will take an interest in what they are doing if they are with me."

"Well, if that's the case, they're obviously up to no good, and so I'm glad they don't want to know you!" I said with more anger than intended.

I really felt for him when he told me how, when he first met them, they called him a mummy's boy because he had no father. They dared him to do stupid things, and when he refused, they said he was like a little girl, and started calling him Thomasina. They said he didn't seem much like a man, so he felt he had to do something to prove himself, and when they let him tag on to their gang, he was ready to do anything to gain their respect. This was why he'd hit out at the police officer, thinking this would impress them; but at the first hint of trouble they had run off and left him to carry the can. Poor Tom, it seemed like his efforts to prove he was grown-up had only managed to highlight his immaturity.

Once I had broached the subject of the move, I actually felt much better, and although we were not yet in agreement, Tom did appear mildly interested, and I was a lot more optimistic than I had been at the beginning. Encouraged by his lack of opposition, I decided to play my best shot.

"If you really don't want to continue your education, perhaps you could find a job in Norfolk. I've heard there are a lot of opportunities in agriculture and horticulture if that's what you want to do, and once you finish your exams, I will be happy if you are doing something you are really interested in."

That did it; although he didn't immediately agree, I knew I had won him over when he started to ask about the cottage and the village. At first quite hesitantly, but then with increasing enthusiasm, he wanted to know more about it, and for the first time in many months we actually talked. As I looked at this boy who was growing up before my eyes, I couldn't help wondering about the family he resembled. I had never attempted to trace my origins, nor would I, for after Richard's attack when for a long while I thought I was in some way to blame, I feared that finding my real parents might confirm what I already suspected: that I came from bad stock — for why else would they have given me away? However, when I looked at Tom, I realised that whoever they were, they must have had some good in them, for so much of this boy must have come from them, and he was very special. I was suddenly awash with the guilt of all the lies I had told to cover up his origins, but knew that they were for his benefit and did no harm, and so pushed it to the back of my mind again. As I answered all of Tom's questions as best as I could with the limited memory I had of the cottage, I realised that with remarkable ease, the way was clear and the move a reality.

Chapter 5
NEW BEGINNINGS

Once the decision had been made, it was surprising how smoothly everything went. After another conversation with the solicitor, I discovered that the cottage had been left untouched, and so I made arrangements for a house clearance firm to collect the key from the solicitor, clear the house completely and just send me a cheque for the proceeds. I certainly didn't want any of my parents' personal belongings, and although I hadn't much in the way of furniture, I was determined not to have anything that brought back the past; and anyway, a fully furnished house complete with clothes and personal items would have taken some explaining to Tom.

The next step was to take him to see the empty property, so I arranged a day off from work to coincide with one of his study days, and turned the viewing into an outing, albeit without much studying! I did insist he brought some revision with him to work on during the journey, but the drive from Essex to Norfolk took in some lovely scenery and he spent more time gazing out of the window than actually revising. As we started travelling through picturesque villages and country lanes, Tom became more and more enthusiastic, and was obviously looking forward to seeing the cottage. However, when we finally arrived in the right village, he was surprised how easily I found it. Although he knew I had been at least once before to view it, he didn't expect me to find it so easily, as I am not known for my sense of direction, and he said as much.

"It just goes to show that I already feel at home here," I said, and when he saw the cottage nestling behind a huge beech hedge, he had to agree with me. It certainly did have a welcoming appearance, and looked at from the front there was no memory of my headlong run across the fields to the back gate all those years ago. When I had lived there as a child, we never used the front door, always coming around the side and in the back gate, and so this was a view that was nearly as new to me as it was to Tom. The double wooden gates were wide open and gave access to a small parking space in front of the cottage, and as we parked the car and walked up the path to the front door, Tom was immediately impressed with the front garden. Although overgrown and neglected, the variety of shrubs and plants that struggled in what had once been neat borders reminded me that it had once been well cared for, and Tom remarked that whoever had lived here before must have loved their garden. I knew neither of my parents had taken much interest in the garden, but I remembered my grandfather coming and planting stuff, humming away as he lovingly tended them. He was my Dad's father, but didn't look much like him. A small wiry man, completely different from my father's heavy frame, with thin iron-grey hair and brown leathery skin, he always had a smile for me. He would spend time telling me about the flowers he was planting, and the wonderful colours they would be when they came up; but although I tried hard to remember, I had no idea what had happened to him — he just stopped coming one day and no-one mentioned him again. It was clear even from the overgrown state of the present garden that someone must have gone on tending the plants for some time after he stopped coming, but I had no idea who it had been. I realised now that he'd probably died, but I didn't recall a funeral or any grieving, and life just went on as if he'd never been there.

I snapped back to reality and saw Tom's rapt expression as he pushed weeds aside to discover vibrant plants. Growing up in a flat, he'd never had a garden, but from the first time he'd seen cress seeds sprouting on blotting paper a passion for growing things was born. From cress he progressed to house plants and beautiful window boxes, and from about twelve years old he worked in other people's gardens, earning a bit of extra pocket money, but mostly just for the joy of watching things grow. As an avid reader of gardening books and plant and seed catalogues, he'd gained an extensive knowledge over the years, and obviously had a talent to match his enthusiasm. Although I didn't share his interest, I was very impressed with his ability, and proud of the knowledge acquired by his own efforts with no encouragement other than his own passionate interest. As we walked round to the back of the cottage, Tom took one look at the wilderness that was the back garden, and all his previous doubts and indecision seemed to disappear. He was more animated than I had ever seen him, and his only question was, "When?"

I felt buoyed up by his eagerness, and all the soul-searching and anxious worrying I had done before deciding on this momentous step faded into oblivion. I looked at my son, bursting with enthusiasm and happier than I had seen him for weeks, and knew I was doing the right thing.

The bubble burst when I realised that we must look inside the cottage, and I felt the dread in the pit of my stomach, but also a hint of curious excitement. Although the garden seemed more than enough for Tom, I was concerned that he might change his mind when he saw where we were to live. So, with more than a little nervousness, I returned to the front of the cottage and unlocked the front door with the only key I had, and we both walked inside. The cottage smelt musty and unlived in, and the dust-encrusted windows let in little light. The front door opened straight into the living room, and I felt my heart sink when I took in the peeling wallpaper and brown paintwork and realised how much needed doing to make this place anything like homely. Both the front entrance and living room were unfamiliar, as this was a part of the cottage that was rarely used, but I had to hide my feelings from Tom and try to remain upbeat, as he thought I had already viewed the property, and so I couldn't betray my shock and disappointment. So, forcing myself to sound more cheerful than I felt, I brightly told him that it wasn't anything that a good clean and a coat of paint wouldn't sort out, and to my utter surprise he agreed.

"It won't take long once we get started," he said, "and Oliver's in the High Street has a sale on with all the paint and DIY stuff reduced, so it might not cost too much."

To say I was relieved at his optimism would be an understatement, and his concern for the finances both surprised and touched me, so I tried hard to match his enthusiasm. Once we threw open a few windows and let the sun shine in, lighting up the dancing dust particles, I felt decidedly better and began to see the potential.

The cottage was smaller than I remembered it, but then that could be because I was bigger. The kitchen was just as I remembered, minus the furniture, and I was both surprised and pleased to find the back-door key still in the door so that I could open this up and let some more light and air in. The bathroom was also on the ground floor and that was exactly as it had been, and for a moment I was back trying to wash the smell and taste of Richard from me in this tiny space without anyone finding out. I did not dwell long in this space and strode determinedly back into the kitchen and opened the door to the steep winding stairway. When we arrived at the top of the stairs and I looked at what had been my bedroom, I was amazed to see how tiny it was. Although it was many years since I had slept in this room, I recognised the rosebud wallpaper, and realised with a hint of sadness that nothing had changed since I had left. It would be nice to think they were keeping it for my return, and yet I knew this wasn't the case and it was more likely that they had just shut the door and forgotten I existed. I couldn't help wondering what was in here when the men came to clear it, and if they went off with my childish drawings and scribblings tucked in the drawers, or my school uniform still hanging in the wardrobe. The larger bedroom that had belonged to Mum and Dad was also much as I remembered it, but I immediately decided that this would be Tom's room. It wasn't just that he would never have enough space for his record collection, books and catalogues in the smaller room, but also because I knew I would never feel comfortable sleeping in a room that even now, empty, still seemed like it belonged to them.

When we had seen all there was to see, we shut the windows again and locked up the cottage. We were both lost in our own thoughts and set off on the journey home in silence, but then hunger broke into our reverie and by mutual agreement we stopped for fish and chips. It was then that we started talking and began to realise that this move was actually going to happen, and surprisingly it seemed that we were both actually looking forward to it.

This visit set the pattern for the weeks to come, which flew by in a whirl of activity, shopping for paint and curtain material and driving up to Norfolk most weekends to decorate and prepare our new home. We became much closer as we planned the changes, and for the first time in a long while, I realised we were actually talking and laughing together like we used to do before Tom went off the rails. I was happier than I had been since Nan had died, and really enjoyed our trips to Norfolk and the changes that were happening before our eyes. While I was concentrating on the inside, Tom had already cut a path through the overgrown garden, and had discovered a wealth of plants and shrubs that began to thrive in their newly cleared environment. When we were in Essex, all his thoughts and conversation were now about the move, and his obvious enthusiasm when he spoke of his plans for the garden was lovely to see. I was relieved that he didn't attempt to pick up with the old crowd, and although with exams in full swing he had to find some time for revision, we still managed to get to Norfolk most weekends.

When the day arrived to leave the Essex flat that had been home for most of Tom's life, and the most important part of mine, I was sick with worry. Was I doing the right thing? How was I going to cope if Tom hated it and wanted to come home? What if I hated it and wanted to come home? I realised I was still thinking of the flat as home even though, after today, I would never step into it again, and that thought made my stomach do cartwheels. Tom seemed to have no such concerns or regrets about leaving, as he rushed around checking the empty rooms and chattering on about the cottage and the garden, more to himself than to me. Once we had packed the last few bits into my elderly Vauxhall Victor, he jumped into the passenger seat without a backward glance, but I locked the door of the flat for the last time with a feeling of sadness. The small furniture van had left about half an hour before, packed with our furniture, including a few new bits and pieces that I'd managed to buy out of the proceeds from the sale of the old stuff. Luckily, Tom didn't ask where the money had come from, but then, like most sixteen-year-olds, he'd little interest in finance and assumed there would always be enough, despite me constantly telling him it didn't grow on trees. I expected the journey to take around two hours, but the van would be slower, so by my calculations we would arrive at about the same time. As I headed back to the village where I had grown up, I couldn't help remembering the journey in the opposite direction all those years ago, sitting silent and afraid next to the stiff-backed form of my father, and then I realised with a sudden pang of sadness that was the last time I had seen him.

Chapter 6
MOVING ON

Other than a lack of light bulbs and a cracked vase, the move went smoothly enough, and when I finally closed the door on the removal men and put the kettle on, we both breathed a sigh of relief. I had planned to go out for an evening meal in the local town, but now we were in with a cup of tea in our hands, it all seemed a bit of an effort, so I raided the boxes to see what I could find. My search turned up a tin of chicken soup, some bread and cheese and a couple of packets of crisps, which, after a long, hungry day, seemed like a banquet, so we settled for a picnic meal on the kitchen table, washed down with more tea. When we had finished, Tom jumped up, and without a word disappeared upstairs. After a moment or two, he returned with a large bottle of cider.

"I thought we might celebrate," he said, looking a bit sheepish, and although I was curious, I decided to accept the offer without enquiring into its source.

It felt very strange to be sitting in this kitchen again after so many years, and I found myself drifting back; but I really didn't want to dwell on the past, so I turned my attention to the cider and asked Tom about his plans for the garden. This opened the floodgates and Tom was soon in full flow, enthusiastically describing his ideas in detail. I was able to listen without comment, as he hardly took time to draw breath.

"The garden is packed full of plants already," he said. "I know lots of them, but there are a few I haven't seen before and I'll have to look them up. The trouble is they can't breathe, so I'll clear away all the rubbish and give them more of a chance to grow. There're some lovely old-fashioned rose bushes, and some peonies, I think, but until I can clear away the weeds, I've no idea what else I might find. I think we might both be surprised with just how many plants we have out there."

Although I nodded in agreement, I didn't think I would be at all surprised, for even after all these years I could remember vividly the lovely cottage garden where I had played as a tiny girl and soaked up the sun in later years. Tom's voice interrupted my thoughts as he continued.

"What would be really nice is a wildlife pond, something to attract the frogs and encourage water plants," he said almost to himself, and then, warming to his subject, "Perhaps I could rig up a fountain or waterfall. I love the sound of running water in a garden."

He didn't seem to require any response, and went on without waiting for answers; but when he eventually ran out of steam, he looked at me as if seeking my approval. My heart went out to him: I hadn't seen him this excited since he was a small boy and his enthusiasm was infectious, and I felt myself looking forward to the beautiful garden-to-come with almost as much excitement.

"Well, I think it sounds great. I'd better invest in some garden chairs so we can sit out and admire our lovely garden. We'll be able to sit in the sun with a cool drink and listen to the fountain. I can hardly wait!" And on that happy note we cleared away the dishes and headed for bed.

After a good night's sleep, no doubt due to total exhaustion, I woke up to the sun streaming in through the low window and with a growing sense of contentment. For the first time since I had started planning this crazy idea, I was sure it had been the right decision, and we really would make a new life which would be better for both of us. I almost leapt out of bed filled with a sense of purpose and determination, and when I joined Tom in the kitchen, it was obvious he felt the same way. Still bursting with excitement, he decided to take a bike ride round the village to find his bearings. Although I was tempted to tell him to wait for me, I realised he needed to find his own feet without Mum in tow, so sent him off with a cheery wave, but also a warning to be careful, as I had done since he was a small boy. I realised after he left that this probably wasn't necessary as he was hardly likely to meet much in the way of traffic and he was almost seventeen, but it made me feel better. Once he'd left, I was content to take a breather and enjoy the cottage, which now bore little resemblance to my childhood home. The heavy curtains in the kitchen, which never seemed to let in any light, had changed to bright yellow and white check, tied back with white ribbon, which I thought far more suitable for a cottage. Similarly, the oversized wooden table and rather ornate chairs, which was the scene of my shame in the face of my father's wrath, always seemed rather out of place in a cottage kitchen. These had gone off with the house clearance company and given way to a pine refectory table with upholstered pine benches. The bright lemon walls were a definite improvement on the previous mustard, and a rush mat running the length of the flagstone floor scrubbed clean of years of wear completed the dramatic improvement. The cupboard doors had a fresh coat of yellow paint with white surrounds, and new white handles had taken the place of the old wooden ones. A toaster, washing machine and coffee percolator brought the kitchen up to date, and a portable radio completed the picture. I was very proud of the transformation, and the rest of the small cottage had benefitted from similar treatment. Tom and I had worked very hard to bring this cottage up to date, and we had every reason to feel proud of our efforts. Determined to wipe away all traces of the past, we had systematically gutted each room, scraping off old wallpaper and ripping up old carpets. The little-used sitting room had been kept as almost a shrine to the long-dead Thomas Michael, and I took a guilty pleasure in erasing all memories of the child who, through no fault of his own, had blighted my young life. As I stood on the threshold of this room now, I recalled the upright piano that no-one ever played, but which was covered in baby photos in ornate silver frames, and the heavy velvet curtains which were rarely opened more than a few inches. I could only ever remember the fire alight at Christmas, and I think that was the only time that the three of us ever sat together in this room. Although all the furniture had gone before we started working on it, the room remained musty and dark as the curtains and carpet were still in place, and this was the first thing that had to change. Once these were disposed of and the windows opened up, it was obvious that this could actually be a beautiful room. With its south-facing window, it was naturally sunny during the day, and the large chimneybreast and open fireplace promised cosy nights in winter. The pastel pink emulsion I chose for the walls with the white ceiling and paintwork immediately brightened the whole room. The addition of a modern three-piece suite, coffee table and a television set brought it smack up to date, and the new gold carpet and curtains were the final addition. Both Tom and I were very pleased with this room, although Tom was less than impressed when I added my own array of baby photos.

The old sixties bathroom had given me a few headaches; as I had spent so much money and effort on the rest of the cottage, I really couldn't afford either the expense or the time to rip out the fittings, even though they were very old fashioned. However, as luck would have it, I came across a magazine article on revamping old bathrooms and used many of the ideas to improve the rather cheerless room, which now sported a shower with bright shower curtain and matching blind, some attractive new tiles round the walls and a vinyl-covered floor complete with fluffy bath mat.

Tom's bedroom had been brought sharply into the eighties with posters, portable TV and stereo in addition to the rather outlandish colour scheme which he insisted on; but I had kept my room simple, with cream walls and carpet and rose-coloured curtains, bedspread and scatter cushions. As I wandered around the cottage contemplating all our hard work, I couldn't help trying to imagine my parents in the newly modernised cottage; but, try as I might, I couldn't put them in the picture. They had always seemed tired and dull even when they had been relatively young, and their sad and melancholy nature made them somehow belong in the dark and dingy surroundings that they had made no effort to change. It was only now, many years later, that I realised how oppressive my home had been, and I understood what had drawn me to the bright and cheerful surroundings of Jess's house. The tragic irony was that a child's need for a more homely atmosphere had resulted in an abrupt and violent end to childhood. I banished the thought as soon as it entered my mind, as I was determined to look forward and not back — this was my chance to make a new life and put my demons to rest. I suddenly realised with a sense of satisfaction that here, in the bright and homely kitchen, I had really begun to feel at home.

Now it only remained for me to venture out, and so I decided to take a walk to the local shop while Tom was out, pick up a few groceries and light bulbs and see how the village had changed in the seventeen years since I had left. Despite my new-found strength, I was still anxious about going into the village in case anyone recognised me; but I need not have worried, as I soon discovered that the village appeared to have changed almost as much as I had, and I doubted if any of the original residents were still there. A small new development of bungalows had sprung up along the lane, and the village school now had portable classrooms in the playground, presumably to accommodate the increased population. Other new houses dotted the village street and there was evidence of a new kind of villager, with garden gnomes, Grecian urns and palatial birdhouses. Some of them sported five-bar gates or leaded windows in an effort to appear rustic, but the ornate lamp-posts, coloured stepping-stones and fanciful house names rather gave the game away. It seemed that we were not the only Essex migrants to settle in this part of the country. Beyond the new development were the cottages that I remembered. Some had changed colour and one or two had new windows or doors, but the majority seemed much the same as they had when I was a child. As I walked past the row of cottages, I didn't notice the elderly man pulling up weeds in the small front garden of one of them, and so his cheery "Good Morning" made me jump. Although obviously no longer young, this man retained an almost youthful physique, tall and lean, with no sign of a stoop and a shock of grey hair that had obviously once been dark. There was something vaguely familiar about him and I thought he must have lived in the village when I was there, but I couldn't put a name to him, and he didn't seem to know me, thank goodness, so I wished him Good Morning and carried on walking.

"Are you new to the village or just visiting?" The remark stopped me in my tracks and as I turned to face him, I found myself looking into a pair of smiling blue eyes, which almost seemed too young and vibrant for the leathery brown face, and I knew I had seen them before. This was not only a well-remembered face but a well-liked one as well, and I knew deep down inside me that this man was my friend, and so I relaxed and smiled back at him. I explained that I had just moved into the village with my son, keeping the details sketchy, but he obviously wanted to chat.

"I'm Jack Butler, retired schoolmaster, and I have lived in the village for a long time, so I can say with authority it's a lovely place to live."

Of course — the penny dropped: this was Mr Butler, my inspirational teacher from my very first day at the village school. I remembered how kind he had been, and how fond I had been of him. He'd always seemed to have time for me, and it was his encouragement that had fuelled my passion for writing.

I suddenly realised that I was staring at him and pulled myself together. "I'm sure you're right. I liked the village the first time I saw it, and it's a great change from the bustling town we left behind."

"How old is your son?" he asked. "Will he go to the village school?"

I told him that Tom was almost seventeen, and he said I didn't look old enough to have such a grown-up son. Out of habit, I launched into the dead husband story, although each time I did so lately I felt more guilty about the lies, and especially so with such a kind and genuinely caring man. In an effort to stem any further questions and avoid any more lies, I ended the conversation abruptly, saying that I had to get on. I realised this sounded a little strange coming from a woman with no job and no particular place to go, but hoped that he wouldn't realise that. However, as I walked away, I felt a sense of loss, and regretted that I couldn't renew my friendship with this lovely old gentleman, for fear of pricking his memory and having to tell even more lies.

It was a relief if not a surprise to find the shop in new hands, as I didn't want another trip down memory lane. The couple, who appeared to be the owners, were certainly not locals, but were friendly and helpful. The woman, who introduced herself as Pat, was full of questions, but seemed more interested than intrusive, and I realised that it was quite unusual to have a complete stranger turn up at the village store on foot. I was happy to trot out the customary answers — I had been doing it for so long now that I almost believed in the dead husband myself. I managed to find everything I needed, and put in an order for a daily paper and milk delivery, before saying goodbye and turning to leave. Just as I got outside, I spotted the sign in the window for a part-time post office assistant.

Without time for much thought, I walked back in and asked Pat about the job. She told me that her husband Bob had helped in the shop when they first took over, but now it was up and running he'd found full-time work in the nearby town, as was always the intention, and he would be starting the following Monday. They knew that Pat would need some help with the Post Office, and this was the reason for the advert, but there had been no interest so far, and they were both concerned that she wouldn't be able to cope once she was left on her own. As if on cue, Bob came through from the corn store out the back and Pat introduced him to me. He explained that he'd just managed to find a job with a printing firm in the local town, and as this was his trade, and although worried for Pat, he was looking forward to getting back to work, but they were getting desperate to find some help before he started. Although confident in the shop, Pat was a bit daunted by the Post Office and had relied on Bob for this side of the business; but the thought of taking over and running it herself, was really worrying her. I told them about my banking experience and said I was interested as I needed some part-time work, and they agreed there and then to try me. Although it wasn't too flattering to know they were desperate, it was certainly the easiest job interview I had ever had, and I was confident that I could cope with three mornings a week in the local post office.

They both seemed very nice and they agreed that I could start the following Monday on a trial period to see how I got on, and if all went well, I would be looking after the sub-post office for the three mornings a week that it was open. The hourly rate was quite a bit less than I was getting at the bank, but with my redundancy package and no rent or mortgage to pay, my finances were looking quite healthy, and perhaps I could now write my "bestseller" and have no need to worry about money!

I left the shop feeling elated. Not only had Tom and I settled immediately into our new home, and were getting on so much better, but now I had managed to find a job within walking distance on my first day in the village. I felt a warm feeling inside which spread upwards and put a huge smile on my face, and grinning like some demented Cheshire cat and toting my basket of shopping with me, I headed away from home, and feeling invincible and determined to dispel any demons, I continued up the street towards the end of the village.

Bolstered by a ridiculous sense of self-confidence and a conviction that everything would be fine, I couldn't resist the strange compulsion that drove me on towards the house which I had been so determined to avoid. However, as the tall windows of the grey stone house came into view, all my confidence deserted me, my throat went dry and I felt silly and stupid and couldn't believe I had come here voluntarily. My feet felt like lead, but I kept telling myself it was just a house and I would walk on by with my head in the air and take back the control of my life which had been taken from me all those years ago. I took a deep breath and walked determinedly forward, past the front gate, and I was actually winning the battle when I heard voices that stopped me in my tracks. From the other side of the wall one voice brought memories flooding back; but, even more worryingly, the other voice was definitely Tom's! I could move neither forward nor back, and, rooted to the spot, I couldn't believe what I was hearing. My first instinct was to rush in and "save" my son, but instead I desperately searched my mind for some rational explanation. Perhaps it wasn't Tom, perhaps it just sounded like him. Then I spotted his bike leaning against the wall, and without waiting to hear any more of the conversation, I took the coward's way out, turned on my heels and ran, arriving back at the cottage door, shaking and shivering with terror just as I had seventeen years before.

I seemed to have been sitting at the kitchen table drinking coffee and thinking for hours when Tom burst into the kitchen, but in reality, it was probably no more than half an hour, during which time I had been trying to think what I would say to him and dreading what he may say to me. As it turned out, I need not have worried, for here was my son with a grin from ear to ear telling me that he'd found a job. This was the last thing I expected to hear and, for a moment, I was speechless, not knowing quite how to react. Not understanding my silence, a slightly less exuberant Tom went on to explain that he'd called at the house after reading an advert in the post office window for a gardener. In other circumstances, the coincidence of us both finding a job on the same day from the same source would have been amusing, but the humour was lost in the reality of the situation, and I struggled to gain some composure. In his excitement, Tom didn't seem to notice and went on enthusiastically, telling me he could start the next day, and describing the garden which, without any reminding, I could see as vividly in my mind as the day I had run headlong away from it.

Thinking quickly, I came to an immediate decision. Smiling broadly, I said, "That's wonderful, Tom, well done; and you're not the only one with a new job!" I explained about my trip to the local shop and the offer of the post office job. My performance was worthy of an Academy Award and I managed to convince Tom that I shared his enthusiasm for his new job.

"Well, that's got to be worth celebrating," he said. "I'm starving, what's for lunch?"

I threw together a ploughman's lunch of some lavish proportions and we washed it down with some more of the cider by way of celebration. Even the one glass at that time of day made me feel quite light-headed, so I was happy to drag out the old deckchair I had found in the garden shed and spend the afternoon watching Tom work on the borders. I didn't have to try to make conversation, as Tom was gabbling on about the variety of plants at the big house, and the beautiful walled garden and arches of roses. He didn't seem concerned about my lack of response, or perhaps he didn't notice in his excitement as he hardly had time to draw breath, and I was relieved not to be pressed for answers.

My second night in the cottage was far more restless than the first, and, as I lay staring through the small panes of the low window at the first light of dawn, I felt the same feelings of melancholy and dread that I had experienced in the solicitor's office a few weeks previously. In an effort to pull myself together, I decided to get up and see Tom off to his first day at work with a cooked breakfast and a smile on my face, and despite my inner turmoil, that is exactly what I did.

Chapter 6
FROM TWO TO FIVE

Once he'd gone, I was at a loss to know what to do with myself. The cottage was tidy and the garden was Tom's baby. I wasn't due to start my new job until the following week, and I certainly wasn't used to a life of leisure. Having worked full-time since leaving school as well as bringing up Tom, I'd never had much time for hobbies, and the local paper, which I had heard delivered at the crack of dawn, held little of interest. I decided on a leisurely bath followed by a cup of coffee, but even then, it was still only 9am and the day stretched endlessly ahead. Although my burning ambition to write a bestseller was supposed to come to fruition in this new life, today wasn't the day. I had no ideas and my state of mind wasn't right, as I couldn't seem to concentrate on anything whilst worrying about Tom and his present precarious situation; but I realised that hanging around the house agonising about what might happen wouldn't do anyone any good.

As I returned aimlessly to the local paper, an advert jumped out at me:

Kittens, many colours — parents good hunters — free to good home.

Having discovered evidence of mice in the garden shed the previous day, and made a mental note that a cat might be the answer, I now had something to do. I was quite excited when I rang the number, and it was good to have something else to occupy my troubled mind. I phoned the number and spoke to a pleasant woman who confirmed that the kittens were still available. She gave me the address, and when she explained where she was, which turned out to be a smallholding in the next village, I remembered seeing it on our trips to the cottage, so I arranged to go and see the kittens straight away. At last, I had a sense of purpose, and putting all other thoughts and worries to the back of my mind, I set about finding an old sweater and a cardboard box. I punched a few holes in the top of the box and took some sticky tape, as I realised it might not be a good idea to try to drive home with a loose kitten in the car. So pleased with my foresight and preparation, especially as I had never owned a cat before, I set off feeling quite excited.

I had always loved animals, and as a child had pleaded with my parents for a pet of my own, but to no avail. I remembered a pretty, if somewhat scruffy, tortoiseshell cat that had wandered in from somewhere and made a home in the shed. Surprisingly, my parents allowed her to stay to control the mice; but, as far as I could remember, they had never fed her or shown any fondness for her, and she felt much the same about humans and wouldn't come near any of us. I tried for weeks with sneaked bits of food to entice her to come to me, but she never would, and then she gave birth to some kittens under the bench in the shed. I was thrilled and excited and made all sorts of plans about taming one of them and making it my pet, but they were there one day and gone the next without ever opening their eyes. I did try to find out what had become of them, but it was only now that I realised that to my parents they were as unwanted as Tom had been later on, but their mother could do nothing to save them. As my parents refused to consider allowing me to have my own pet, I contented myself with looking after other people's while their owners were on holiday. I regularly cared for cats, rabbits, guinea pigs and hamsters, and walked dogs for those that were unable to walk their own. The dogs were my favourite, and I developed an abiding love and affinity with them, as well as discovering a talent for training. One or two of the village dogs learned impressive repertoires of tricks, which left their owners puzzled. One particular Alsatian, as they were called then, decided that I was his new owner and the lady that owned him told me he showed far more excitement when I came round than when she got home. This was probably because other than feeding him and opening the door to the garden, she did nothing at all for the dog, so Teddy — short for Teddy Bear — clearly thought I was more fun. I spent hours of my childhood out with this dog, and this was the one thing I didn't share with Jess, who never showed any interest in animals. I wondered what had happened to Teddy, and for the first time since being shipped unceremoniously off to Essex, I thought about how he must have felt when I disappeared from his life so abruptly. I was too scared and miserable to miss him, but I'm sure he must have felt bewildered by my absence, and I suddenly realised that, other than a quick pat of a stranger's dog, or a stroke of a neighbour's cat over the years, I hadn't had any contact with animals since the last time I'd taken Teddy out.

Full of excited anticipation, I found the smallholding without any difficulty and pulled into the yard. The property was more like a garden centre, with flowers and plants for sale and rows of greenhouses along the roadside. In an adjoining paddock there were a few sheep and a couple of goats, and outside in the yard an assortment of ducks, chickens and geese were wandering about. As soon as my car entered the gateway, a group of scruffy barking sheepdogs rushed round the wheels and I wasn't sure whether it would be safe to get out. However, as soon as I turned off the engine all but one lost interest and went back where they had come from. The one that remained was a youngster, and seemed overjoyed to see me, so I got out of the car and made a big fuss of her. She didn't look any more than six months old, and as she squirmed and wriggled with pleasure at my feet, I forgot all about the kittens, and just wanted to take this delightful little pup home with me. I would have stayed and played with her for longer, but just then the door of the house opened and a man came towards me, and the pup immediately ran off to join its companions, a little too hastily for my liking, and I wondered if she was, in fact, a bit wary of the man, although he seemed okay.

"They're over here in the barn," he said, as he strode off and I scurried to catch up. He pointed to a corner where two black and white kittens were huddled together in a box. I saw no evidence of "many different colours", and it seemed that these two were the only ones available. Although I wasn't an expert, I didn't think they looked much more than four weeks old.

"Do you think they might be a bit too young to leave their mother?" I tentatively suggested.

"The others have all gone and I can't have them hanging about any longer eating me out of house and home."

I didn't think these two looked as if they had eaten much at all, as they were really scrawny, so reasoned that they would be no worse off coming with me. I decided then and there that I couldn't leave one on its own and I would have to have them both, so Rosie and Daisy (in honour of their origins) were duly loaded into the cardboard box and sealed up ready for the journey home. I was just about to leave when I felt the wistful eyes of the little sheepdog pup watching me. I found myself asking the man about her.

"She was left from the last litter from my Bess and no-one bought her. She don't show no interest in the stock, and so isn't much good for anything, but I'll take a tenner if you're interested."

I was a bit taken aback and I hadn't come with any intention of buying a dog; and much as the pup appealed to me, I was totally unprepared for dog owning. However, the pup's eyes continued to be fixed on me almost as if she knew what was happening, and I could feel myself falling under her spell.

"What's her name?" I asked, stalling for time.

"She don't have no name as I ain't keeping her."

That did it, and I was fishing around in my purse for a ten-pound note without even thinking about it, and Fern (keeping with the flower theme), complete with a collar and lead fashioned from baling twine, joined Rosie and Daisy for the journey home. On the way, I contemplated what I had done — somehow one cat to control the mice had turned into two cats and a dog, and as I'd never owned even one pet before, the prospect of becoming a three-pet family seemed rather like taking on a zoo! However, when I glanced at Fern, sitting happily on the seat next to me as if she'd always belonged, I knew I'd done the right thing, and she'd certainly taken my mind off all my other worries. My next stop would have to be for dog and cat food, but I didn't feel like looking stupid in my own village shop by showing my ignorance of what I needed for my newly acquired pets. I decided instead to stop at the one near the smallholding, which turned out to be identical to the one at home anyway. It appeared to sell just about everything, and it was a safe bet that what they didn't stock they could order. The sub-post office occupied one corner of the small shop and an outside store was home to every kind of animal feed. Unfortunately, the choice of dog and cat food was mind-blowing, with canned, bagged and loose food and labels claiming it promoted a glossy coat, energy and health. I played safe and bought cans of dog and cat meat and some mixer biscuits, and felt, even with no experience, it didn't look too complicated. At least I wouldn't have to guess how much to give them, as there were some useful charts on both the cans and the mixer. I chose what looked on the labels like the tastiest brands, although I was aware that this was hardly scientific or necessarily sensible, but reasoned I would learn as I went along. I remembered to buy some cat litter and a tray, although not entirely sure where I had heard about these, but knew I would need them. I was about to go back into the shop to pay for it all when I saw the stand with the collars and leads on, and a picture of the baling twine flashed in my mind. I knew I could do better than that, and when I spotted a nice red leather collar and matching lead, I had no hesitation adding it to my load. As I walked back into the shop, I glanced back at the car and saw Fern's little face with her nose pressed firmly against the window, watching my every move. I felt a warm glow inside which overcame all my doubts, until I stepped back inside the shop, and stepped back in time, for there in front of me was Jess.

Despite the seventeen-year gap, I had no doubts that this was indeed my old friend, for other than added height and a few more curves, she had hardly changed. Wisps of her unruly sandy hair were escaping from the ribbon that tied it back, and despite a valiant attempt at make-up, a mass of freckles still covered her face. I had an almost uncanny feeling that I had met this grown-up woman before, and then realised that Jess was the image of her mother, and thankfully bore no resemblance to Richard.

I must have been staring and Jess suddenly became aware of me, so I quickly looked away and became very interested in the *Woman and Home* magazine on the display in front of me. I thought I saw a brief flicker of recognition in Jess's eyes before I turned away, but thankfully she said nothing and left the shop without looking back. I heard the shopkeeper say goodbye to Jess and then suddenly realise that she had left her purse on the counter. Turning to her little girl, she told her to run after Mrs Hughes and give her back her purse, so I realised with surprise that Jess was married. I don't know why this surprised me, but I suppose I still thought of her at fourteen years old and living in the big house, even though I was all grown up. I guessed she must live fairly close as she wasn't driving a car, and I fought the urge to run after her and give her a big hug. My mind was in turmoil — how could I have hoped to come back here and not meet anyone I knew? I had been very naive in thinking there would be no problems and no-one would find out my secret, and in just the first two days of my new adventure all my carefully thought-out plans had gone wrong. Not only was my son actually working for the one person I had tried to protect him from, but now I had come face to face with Jess, who could blow my cover and give the game away to Tom. Despair flooded over me and I walked back to the car with a feeling of impending disaster. Fern, however, had no such feelings and greeted me as if I'd been away for weeks. I couldn't remain serious in the face of the sheer enthusiasm of this little dog, and found myself laughing as I made a fuss of her. I started to hope that things might not be as bad as I feared, so I decided to look on the bright side. Nothing had happened so far, and perhaps nothing ever would. Then on the drive home the devil tapped me on the shoulder and told me I must go back. I would have to sell the cottage and move back to Essex before it all came crashing down on my head. With a rising sense of panic, the questions filled my head. What could I tell Tom? What could I do with two newly acquired kittens and a little dog? What about my job? No, I pushed the devil aside and decided to remain optimistic and deal with whatever came along.

When I got back to the cottage, I pushed all my worries to the back of my head, as I was much too busy settling the animals to think about my problems; and by the time I'd fed the kittens and put a cardboard box and a blanket with their litter tray in the shed, I felt better. I'd recovered from the shock of seeing Jess and decided to try to forget the incident; after all, she obviously lived in that other village and I would never need to go back there, and so would probably never see her again. While I was busy with the kittens, Fern had never been far away from me, and I suddenly remembered the nice new collar and lead. They lay on the kitchen table where I had dumped all my shopping, but I was quite surprised to discover that putting the collar round Fern's neck wasn't going to be as easy as I imagined. While she was very happy to grab it, chew it or run off with it, she had no intention of wearing it; but after a lot of wriggling and rolling on her back, she was duly "collared". She was none too happy with the sensation and ran around the room pawing at her neck, scratching and whining, which Rosie and Daisy found highly amusing when they crept in through the open back door to watch the entertainment. Without any sign of fear, they chased her around the room as if it was all some game laid on for their benefit, but Fern was oblivious to them as she desperately tried to rid herself of this thing around her neck. I did feel sorry for her, but hardened my heart; and then, with a flash of inspiration, I remembered the tennis ball that Tom had found in the undergrowth when clearing the garden.

As soon as I found this and rolled it across the floor, Fern lost interest in the collar and happily chewed and chased the ball round the kitchen, hotly pursued by the two black and white terrors, and I got the definite feeling this wasn't the first such game the trio had played. This new toy kept her occupied for long enough to accept the collar, and then she flopped down under the table and in a few seconds was sound asleep, seemingly unaware of the offending item or the kittens who had settled themselves alongside her.

I felt a pathetic wave of satisfaction; at least something was going right, and I made a mental note to get identity discs engraved for all three as they were already far too precious to risk losing, although I had my doubts about the kittens being content to live in the shed!

Tom arrived home a little less enthusiastically than he'd left that morning. Although delighted with Fern and the kittens, if somewhat surprised at the sudden growth in his family, he seemed a bit distant and far less buoyant than he'd been when he'd left that morning. It was clear that he didn't want to talk about his day, and after a series of yes and no answers, I stopped asking questions. It reminded me of how he'd been in Essex and I hoped it wasn't the start of a return to the sullen uncommunicative boy that had caused me so much anguish. He did let it slip that the boss was hard to please, and I remembered Richard's bullying tactics with his staff of old, and thought it best to change the subject, even though I really wanted to demand how Richard dared to treat my son, and indeed his own, so unkindly. Forcing myself to think more rationally, I suggested we might take Fern for a walk, and Tom readily agreed. The troubles of the day were soon forgotten when we found ourselves doubled up with laughter as Fern tried every trick in the book to disentangle herself from the bright red snake that had attached itself to her collar.

It was a lovely evening and although Fern performed a series of acrobatics, fast runs and stationary protests, she did eventually give in and walk, albeit in fits and starts, at my side; and although there was no conversation, I think we both found the silence pleasant and companionable. Although neither of us knew it, this warm evening stroll was to set the pattern for many more to come, and we returned home feeling relaxed and pleasantly tired. We decided there wasn't anything worth watching on TV, so Tom disappeared upstairs and came down with his customary stack of gardening books and seed catalogues, while I settled down with a good book.

"There is a cream rose bush outside the French windows which has an amazing scent," Tom said, breaking into my consciousness. "I thought I would try to find out what it is, as it would be lovely to have one like it here."

"No!" I almost shouted before I could help myself, as my mind raced back to the time when the scent from those particular roses threatened to suffocate me. Then, seeing Tom's startled face, I added lamely, "I don't like cream roses — they are morbid and make me think of funerals. If we are going to have more roses, let's have red ones!"

Unconvinced, Tom looked questioningly at me, seeing I was quite upset and unable to think why. I knew he must wonder why the mention of cream roses should have had such an effect on me and think it was something from my past. "Is it something to do with the death of your parents? You never speak of them, and I would like to know more about them."

I was immediately on the defensive, making me sharper than I intended. "It's got nothing to do with them, and they have nothing to do with us!" I snapped, and Tom, seeing how angry I appeared to be, obviously thought it best to drop the subject, even though it was clear he was hurt and confused.

He went back to his books and I returned to mine, and for the next hour or so no word was spoken; but, feeling ashamed of my outburst, I was the first to break the silence and suggested a cup of tea. Tom, relieved to see I was back to normal, put down his books and followed me into the kitchen. Keen to lighten the atmosphere, I asked him to go and check on the kittens, and he returned to report that they had snuggled down together in their bed in the shed, seemingly glad of an early night.

It seems they were not the only ones in need of an early night, and as we sipped our tea, I could feel my eyes getting heavy.

"I think I'll head for bed," I said. "This country air is really having an effect on me."

"Yes, me, too," said Tom.

Fern was fast asleep under the kitchen table and it seemed a shame to wake her, but I knew she must go out if she was going to go through the night, so I woke up the sleepy pup and took her outside. She obliged almost immediately, and as soon as she came back in, she returned to her warm spot and went straight back to sleep. I guessed it had been a stressful day for her, and she was probably worn out.

Taking her cue, I dumped the cups in the sink and followed Tom up the stairs.

However, Fern had different ideas, and as soon as my head touched the pillow, she left me in no doubt of her distress. After getting both Tom and I out of bed on several occasions with pitiful howls, I relented for the sake of peace, and Fern took up what was to be her lifelong sleeping position on the floor at the foot of my bed, from where there wasn't a sound!

Life soon took on a regular pattern. Tom and I ate breakfast together, and then after a quick walk for Fern, we settled her in her bed in the shed. She had access to the garden, which was now securely "dog-proofed", and she had lots of toys to play with, and seemed quite content with this arrangement.

Before long it seemed that Fern had always been with us, and we began to feel much the same about our new life. The walk to work and back was a real pleasure, and even on the days when a brolly or waterproofs were necessary, the wide-open fields and lack of traffic produced a feeling of utter freedom, which I'd never experienced in the busy streets of Chelmsford. Moving as we did at the onset of autumn meant that the countryside was at its most beautiful. The leaves still clung to the trees and bushes, but their various shades of green had given way to richer reds, russets and yellows, and in the early morning the droplets of dew on the ground caught the surrounding colours and shimmered on the grass verge, where my footprints left a clear trail. Since moving back to this lovely village, I had decided to do more walking, both for health and pleasure, and I was looking forward to bright crispy winter mornings with Fern, rediscovering more of the local area where I used to wander as a child.

Although it was clear that Tom wasn't overly keen on his boss, he was still very enthusiastic about his work, and seemed to gain great satisfaction from it. It appeared that Richard carried on much as he'd always done, spending long periods away on business, and at these times Tom seemed far happier to go to work. Within a few weeks of starting, he'd made friends with the young cleaner that came to the house a couple of times a week. Beverley was a local girl whose mother had died of cancer a few years previously, and she now kept house for her father and young sister, taking on the cleaning job to earn a bit of spending money of her own. I could remember both her mother and father from school, although they had been a few years older than me, and I was glad that Tom had found at least one friend in his new home.

My job, as I had expected, wasn't too demanding, but I really enjoyed it. Chatting to the locals was always a pleasure, and even on the rare occasions that they moaned about something, there was often a funny side to it, and we frequently ended up laughing. The customers seemed a lovely bunch, far friendlier than those I was used to in the Essex bank, and several of them had made it their business to find out my name and greeted me as an old friend when they came to buy their stamps or post their parcels. Most of the regulars were elderly and came in every week to collect their pensions. These senior citizens always had time for a chat and I looked forward to their reminiscences. It was a wonderful way to find out all about the village and its inhabitants, as it seemed everyone had time to chat and took pleasure in keeping me well informed. When they talked about the village twenty or more years ago, which they often did, I was transported back in time, and the events and people and even the places they told me about had a nostalgic familiarity, which I secretly enjoyed. I was always especially pleased to see Jack Butler, the chap I'd encountered in his garden on my first walk around the village. Jack was a real gentleman, with a tremendous sense of humour and an obvious joy of life, so I was saddened to hear from Pat that he was terminally ill. She always made a special effort to have time for him, even when she was busy, and I tried to do the same, aware of the fact that he was probably quite lonely, and I'm sure he looked forward to our chats as much as I did. It certainly seemed that the friendship was mutual, and Jack often brought me flowers from his garden and even vegetables when Pat wasn't looking. He always asked after Tom and took interest in what he was doing in the garden, a passion they shared, and he seemed genuinely concerned about how his job at the big house was working out.

One such day, during one of our chats, in walked John Taylor. It was unusual for me to notice him, as I was usually only aware of the customers when they came to my counter; but this young man was particularly striking in appearance, with dark good looks and self-assurance beyond his years. My attention drifted from Jack and I saw that he was arranging with Pat to have a poster displayed in the window. Once he'd finished his business and left, my curiosity got the better of me, and I was unusually impatient for Jack to leave so that I could go and see what the poster said. When he did eventually bid his goodbye, I followed him out to have a look.

"Does your Dog Need Training?" the poster asked.

"Well, yes," I thought.

"Classes on Tuesday nights at the Village Hall by experienced Police Dog Handler."

"He doesn't look old enough to be an experienced anything" crossed my mind, and then I remembered that thinking police officers looked young was a sign of old age, and I couldn't help a giggle.

"I didn't think it was that funny," said a voice behind me, and I spun round to find the young man watching me with an amused smile on his face. For some reason my usually calm demeanour vanished, and I found myself flustered and lost for words. I babbled something about remembering my own dog's silly antics and laughing at them.

"Why don't you bring her along on Tuesday, then? I'm sure my Dad could sort out any problems," he said.

"His Dad," I thought; that explained the "experienced".

"So it's not you who's the policeman, then," I said (missing out the experienced bit!)

"No, I have taken over the Boarding Kennels up the road from my mother, although she still helps out with the grooming business, and Dad is the dog handler, so we are all involved with dogs, and I like to compete in working trials when I get the time."

"Oh, I see," I said, although I didn't; and then, muttering something about seeing if I was free on Tuesday, although obviously I was, in fact, free any evening, I retreated back into the shop feeling unaccountably embarrassed.

Chapter 7
FRIENDS OLD AND NEW

By the time Tuesday evening arrived, it seemed as if I'd thought of nothing else, and after many changes of mind, I decided to give the classes a go. There was no doubt that Fern needed more to do, as no amount of walking or free running appeared to wear her out, and I realised that as a working dog she probably needed more to occupy her mind. So it was with some trepidation that I put Fern's lead on and headed off for the village hall, albeit a little later than I should have been. I had very little idea of what to expect, but I soon found out as I pushed open the door of the hall and pandemonium broke out. Dogs of every shape and size, together with their equally diverse owners, were standing or sitting around the edge of the hall, while a tall grey-haired man struggled with an over-exuberant Boxer in the middle of the room. As this rowdy young hooligan lunged to the end of his lead, causing other dogs in the room to bark and yap at him, the man called the dog's name, took one step back and, with something obviously tasty concealed in his hand, had the dog's attention and praised him. I was very impressed, and decided that here was a man who really knew what he was doing. However, I wasn't sure Fern was as impressed as I was, as she huddled silently in a heap at my feet, looking anything but confident.

Once the assembled gathering had settled, the trainer introduced himself as Doug and told us a bit about himself. He was a police dog handler and had been in the force for almost twenty years. His work dog was called Kane and he was still fairly new to the job, having just taken over from the old dog Dax. Doug brought Kane in to meet everyone, and he obviously enjoyed being the centre of attention. A big black and gold German Shepherd dog whose size belied his youth, Kane still retained a puppy-like exuberance, and I was amazed at how friendly he was. I'd imagined that he would be aggressive, but Doug took time to explain that a good police dog must have a super-friendly and fearless temperament, and there was no doubt that Kane fitted the bill.

Once Kane was returned to the van outside, Doug introduced his son John, who would act as his assistant, and they started to get to know us. Doug suggested that we all took turns in introducing our dogs and ourselves to the class and talking about what we hoped to achieve. I felt an inexplicable blush when my turn came, and explained I'd never owned a dog before, but thought that Fern needed something to do, and I was quite interested to find out more about training; and with a flash of inspiration that I thought would impress, I added that perhaps I might even like to compete. I have no idea where that came from, and didn't dare look at John in case he guessed it was something to do with him, a thought I wouldn't even admit to myself. Once the training started, I was surprised to find how much I enjoyed it, which may have had a lot to do with Fern's ecstatic joy over everyone and everything. Doug was patient and explained the reasons behind every instruction, and even some of the less likely candidates surprised their owners by responding to the positive training methods, which they were able to understand. The boxer, now back in his owner's hands, seemed fascinated by Doug, who had obviously made quite an impression on him, and so enthralled was he watching what was going on that he sat quietly taking it all in, which was a vast improvement on his earlier behaviour.

Fern was a joy to train as she seemed delighted with the attention and quickly picked up whatever I was trying to show her. As soon as Doug showed us all how to hold the lead and motivate our dogs, Fern was happy to trot at my side, looking up into my face and wagging her tail with delight. She didn't pull or take any interest in what was going on around her, but just seemed to enjoy being with me and loving whatever we were doing. When the time came for my turn to walk Fern round the hall on my own, despite being a bit self-conscious, I was really proud of how well she was doing, and I soon forgot my nerves and just enjoyed showing her off. Doug congratulated everyone on their progress and told us to keep practising the things we'd been shown until we met again the following week. As we were preparing to leave, John made his way over to me and told me how well we'd done. He said that Fern was a natural and if we went on at this rate then competition was definitely a possibility. I felt myself blush yet again when I remembered with embarrassment my opening speech about wanting to compete, without any idea of what I was talking about. John seemed not to notice as he made a tremendous fuss of Fern, who obviously thought this new friend was great.

"You should give some thought as to what direction you want to take her in," he said. "She is much too good to waste, and whether you choose to do obedience competitions or working trials, she is about ready for some formal training."

Although I had never heard of either of these, I realised that obedience competition sounded self-explanatory, but I had no idea what working trials were, although it seemed to sound like something gundogs or sheepdogs would do. My enthusiasm over Fern and a need to know more overcame my initial shyness and I didn't hesitate to launch into conversation.

"I think I know about obedience competitions," I said. "There used to be a dog show on the park near us in Essex and I have seen dogs walking to heel, recalling and retrieving like your Dad was telling us about; but what are working trials? Are they something to do with sheep or guns?"

John launched into his subject with passion and took time to explain the rudiments of the discipline. He told me I wasn't the first to confuse working trials with sheepdog or gundog trials, but this was something quite different.

"Working trials are about as close as the ordinary person gets to working their dog for real," he said. "The individual exercises are very similar to police work, with tests in tracking and searching, as well as both obedience and agility. It is great fun, but takes up a lot of time and demands a lot of commitment; but if you are interested, we could start Fern on it and see what you think."

This sounded really interesting, but I was honest enough to admit to myself that watching paint dry could sound really interesting if explained with such enthusiasm by such an attractive young man. This thought made me smile, and John seemed to read this as acceptance.

"You will not be able to teach Fern the working trial exercises at classes, as most of the work needs to be done outside; but if you have a couple of spare evenings a week, you and Fern could join me and my two dogs for training sessions. We have plenty of land around the kennels and I'm sure we could get her started and see what you think."

I noted with some degree of irony that I actually had all my evenings spare as I had no real friends since moving to the village and nowhere much to go, and I had certainly enjoyed myself at the class and looked forward to doing some more. John said we needed to keep up the obedience training and suggested that I carried on going to classes, but trained with him in between. I liked the sound of this, not least, as I had to admit to myself, because I so much enjoyed John's company, but also because this new activity sounded so interesting.

"Why don't you come along to the kennels tomorrow evening if you are free, and we'll make a start on seeing what this little girl can do?"

"Okay," I said as casually as I could, but the unexpected rush of excitement as I said it took me by surprise.

From such casual and vague beginnings, these meetings soon became a regular thing, and with my work at the post office, classes at the village hall and lessons at the kennels, my life settled into an enjoyable and somewhat busy routine. I had not seen any more of Jess and guessed that she rarely came to our village, although I thought it a little strange if she didn't visit her father. It appeared all my earlier fears had come to nothing, and although I knew his job had its drawbacks, Tom seemed to have found his feet in other ways. He had obviously settled in and made some friends, and although I saw much less of him, it was clear he was happy and I could relax, safe in the knowledge he was doing okay. As the weeks passed Fern blossomed; she got on really well with John's two collies, Trim and

Twig, and very quickly began to pick up the basics of working trials. There seemed no end to her ability to learn, or her enthusiasm, and I think John found this as exciting as I did. As the weekly obedience classes progressed, some of the dogs and handlers seemed to lose interest and disappear, while others showed great improvement, but none more so than Fern, who was like a sponge, soaking up the training and always ready for more. John told me that although some of the improvement was down to Fern's own enthusiasm and ability to learn, some was also down to me.

"No amount of training can take the place of natural talent, which you certainly have, and together with your enthusiasm, which is almost as great as Fern's, you two are bound to do well."

I still enjoyed the training classes at the village hall, not least because John was always there helping when needed with difficult dogs, and offering advice to handlers in between sessions. Fern seemed to enjoy this every bit as much as the more complicated stuff she did at the kennels, and I sometimes helped at the class as well by showing things that Fern could do, so spent quite a bit of time with John. I found him so easy to talk to and, possibly because of his age, he didn't put me on my guard as so many men did, so I totally let down my defences. I told myself that there was no way a man of twenty would be interested in me at almost thirty-two, so I could relax and get to know him without the fear of complications. John was very keen for Fern and I to start competing and wanted me to go along to a trial with him so I could see what it was all about. I was becoming more interested, especially as Fern was showing such promise, and so when John told me he was competing in a trial the following weekend, I agreed to go with him.

The day at the trial was magical. I had no idea I would enjoy it so much, and even though the weather was cold and drizzly, the friendly atmosphere and the thrill of watching the skill of the handlers and ability of the dogs made the day fly by. John qualified his young dog in one of the lower stakes and was very pleased, and although I didn't really understand the significance of a qualification, I was very happy to share his enjoyment. I found watching the work very exciting, and was starting to get an idea of the requirements and faults, but couldn't quite imagine doing it myself. However, when I remembered how well Fern was doing the more elemental exercises, the thought of us competing didn't seem so far-fetched, and I found myself wondering if Fern would be able to manage the six-foot scale and nine-foot long jump, both essential parts of the Agility Section.

As John was presented with his certificate of qualification at the end of the day, I felt so pleased and proud, but then couldn't help wondering why. I had nothing to do with his training, or contributed in any way to his success, and yet I had to admit I had become very close to him over the past few weeks. We shared the same zany sense of humour, love of dogs and an affinity that went beyond casual friendship, and with a jolt I realised that not only did I look forward to seeing him, but I couldn't imagine life without him. I was appalled, but no matter how much I tried to tell myself that this was an innocent friendship with no commitment or involvement, I suddenly realised that it simply wasn't true. This was brought firmly home to me when one of the young lady competitors ran up to give John a congratulatory kiss and in the pit of my stomach, I felt a pang of what could only be described as jealousy! Summoning up all the self-control that I had been forced to learn at the age of thirteen, I also went forward to offer congratulations to John.

"It's customary to get a kiss," he said, and I felt myself blush crimson as I planted a peck on his cheek.

The journey home was charged with electric; as we drove, the conversation became more and more intense. It seemed that neither of us was ready to speak openly about our feelings, but I think we both knew that there was something happening between us. Since the abrupt and brutal end to any sexual fantasies I may have experienced before I was attacked, I was suddenly aware of stirrings that I had never expected to feel again. This man was affecting me as no man had before, and I was both excited and afraid, feeling like a schoolgirl with a crush, but with a depth of passion far beyond that of adolescence.

John was the first one to broach the subject of his feelings in his usual candid fashion.

"Rachel," he said, "we have become very good friends and I love being with you, but I think we both know there is more to it than that."

I didn't know what to say or how to react; breathing had become difficult, my heart was thumping in my chest, and I could feel the colour rushing to my cheeks, so to cover my embarrassment, I resorted to humour.

"Well, yes, of course; you're the dog trainer and I'm your pupil, although that makes me sound like the dog!" I replied with a giggle.

"Why are you avoiding the issue, Rachel? You know what I'm talking about. Sometimes you seem so afraid, almost like a butterfly trapped in a jar, beating your beautiful wings against the glass. I would really love to set you free."

I was totally overwhelmed and really touched by this unexpectedly gentle declaration which brought tears to my eyes, but I tried to keep the conversation light-hearted.

"I'm a bit too clumsy to be a butterfly. I think Tom might say more like a dragonfly!" Then, suddenly serious and somewhat defensive, I went on, "I really don't know what to say, or what you want from me. I'm not about to jump into bed with you, you know." As soon as the words were out of my mouth, I regretted both the harshness and the content. Why did I say that? Talk about having a high opinion of yourself. Whatever would he think of me? However, his reply took me completely by surprise.

"Why not?" he said. "It doesn't sound like a bad idea to me," and although he softened the words with a smile, I was totally shocked.

Unsure whether his frankness was due to youth or arrogance, I certainly hadn't expected this answer, and really didn't know what to say. The age gap yawned between us, and I grabbed at it to use as a barrier. "Don't be ridiculous; you're not much older than Tom!"

"Age is just a collection of numbers," he replied. "And anyway, please correct me if I'm wrong, but I don't think your feelings for me are maternal. In fact, if you'd just let your guard down for one moment, you would realise that what we feel for each other has nothing to do with age."

Gone was the easy friendship, replaced by a restraint borne of apprehension on my part, and a sort of kindly mild amusement whenever John looked my way. A part of me wanted to throw caution to the wind, fall into his arms and hold on to him forever; but my more sensible adult side was telling me to run away and put a stop to this complication in my life. In the end I said nothing, and just sat trying to control my thumping heartbeat and churning stomach.

Without any sort of plan, on the way back we pulled in at a small pub that served food to get a bite to eat, but when we'd settled ourselves at a table with a drink and the menu, it seemed that neither of us was hungry. We sat gazing blankly at the menu, sipping our drinks in silence; but when we both looked up at the same time and caught each other's eye, we just burst out laughing and joined hands across the table. Although I felt a sudden rush of happiness as our hands touched, I couldn't help feeling that the whole bar was staring at the older woman seducing the young man. Then it occurred to me that in this place, so far from home, I didn't care, and for a brief moment I just enjoyed the thrill of physical contact which took me completely by surprise.

When we arrived back at the cottage, it was quite late and Tom had obviously gone to bed. I toyed with the idea of asking John in for coffee, but realised that this idea was fraught with danger, so I used the animals as an excuse to go straight in. After all the goodbyes and thanks, I got Fern out of the back of the car and she ran up the path ahead of me. As I turned to leave, I felt John's hand on my arm and, despite all my misgivings, I half-turned back to him and was kissed firmly but tenderly on the lips. I quickly pulled away, and yet everything inside me wanted to stay and fall back into his arms. I almost jumped out of the car and ran up the path, but when I reached the front door I couldn't resist turning back, and there sat John, smiling at me and blowing kisses, and almost against my better judgement I found myself smiling back before I turned to go inside.

I spent a very restless night, but in the cold light of dawn, my rational side had made a decision. I would stop the classes and see no more of John; and although my spirits sank and a feeling of depression swept over me, I was nevertheless sure that this was the right thing to do. My mind made up, I got up and, together with Fern, went downstairs to face the day. Tom was up ahead of me and about to leave for work, but as I didn't start until 9am, I wasn't in any hurry. Tom swilled down the last of his coffee. "You were late back last night," he said, making me feel like a naughty teenager. "Did you have a good time?"

I went for the casual non-committal, but the colour that swept up from my neck belied my words. However, thankfully Tom wasn't paying much attention, and grabbing his packed lunch from the fridge, he was out of the back door and away. Noticing the empty bottle on the table, I went to the front door to see if the milk had arrived. I was amazed to find that the milk wasn't the only thing on the doorstep — lying next to the two bottles was a spray of carnations with a note attached that just said, "Thank you for a lovely day." As I picked them up, I noticed the butterfly, a tiny but perfect drawing in the corner of the card. I swallowed hard and felt my eyes fill with tears.

The morning at work dragged on with very few customers, but just as I was about to cash-up and leave, I heard my name.

I had been so engrossed in cashing-up the post office that I hadn't noticed anyone come into the shop, so the voice made me jump.

"Rachel — it is Rachel, isn't it? I'd know you anywhere!" and I looked up into the face of Jess.

Not waiting for an answer, she went on, "I was sure it was you a few weeks ago in my local shop, but you didn't speak; and then you were gone, so I thought I was wrong, but now I know it's you — don't you remember me? It's me — Jess."

I was stunned, but desperate to prevent anyone hearing her, so I told her I would meet her outside in ten minutes, and hustled her out of the shop. Although clearly puzzled, she did as I asked and waited for me to finish and join her. I was frantically trying to think what to do, as I struggled to make sense of the cashing-up procedure. Luckily, it had been a very quiet morning and so not much to count, although a part of me wished it could take much longer and delay the inevitable questions which I didn't know how to answer. All too soon, I was walking through the door and towards Jess's car.

"Come back with me and have some lunch," she said as soon as I reached her open window. "It's not far, and I can bring you back later."

I thought about using Fern as an excuse to go straight home, but I knew , that even though she was now trustworthy enough to be left in the kitchen she still had access to the back garden so she would be fine and, despite all my fear and apprehension, I realised that I still felt the familiar fondness for this old friend that the years hadn't diminished. Our enforced parting all those years ago had left me feeling bereft at the time, and the hole that remained had never fully healed. I hadn't been that close to anyone since, and although I had acquaintances, colleagues and even friends over the years, none of them made up for the close friendship and the happy times we two had shared.

As I climbed into the car beside her, Jess leaned across and hugged me with a spontaneity that was so natural and warm I just instinctively knew that everything would be all right.

"Oh, Ellie," she said, "it is so good to see you. I have missed you so much, and always wondered what had happened to you. Where have you been?"

"It's a very long story, Jess," I said, automatically slipping back into the familiar nickname which she always used, but immediately realising that I must not be known as Ellie anymore, so I told her that I preferred Rachel now.

"Well, you must tell me all about it, and I will try to remember to call you Rachel — but first, I will tell you about me."

It seemed Jess had gone away to a private boarding school shortly after I had left the village. She didn't say why, but reading between the lines I got the definite impression that it was at her own request and assumed she just wanted to get away. Despite her private education, her exam results had been disappointing, and there was no more talk of university. Much to her father's disgust, she'd ended up working for a local estate agent both in the office and showing prospective purchasers around vacant properties; and, although she quite enjoyed the job, there were no prospects. However, always one to make the best of a bad situation, Jess had married the boss and now lived quite comfortably in a "detached four-bedroomed country house with en suite master bedroom and ample garden", to quote the agent's details.

"I'm lucky. I don't need to work, so I'm free to do whatever I want," she said, but without much enthusiasm, I thought.

"I like to potter around in the garden and I'm addicted to interior design, but I've done every room in the house now, so will have to find a new project."

Strangely, I found myself feeling sorry for Jess — despite all her apparent comfort, she seemed to be missing something, and I couldn't help feeling, that she was more sad and lonely, than she was telling me, and I wondered just what this husband of hers was like.

So intent was I on Jess's story that I didn't take much notice of where we were, but as we pulled into the sweeping drive, I realised just how rich she and her husband must be. The house was set on a hill, which in itself was a unique feature in flat Norfolk. On each side of the driveway, which climbed to the front of the double garage, rolling lawns covered with randomly planted young trees, like immature parkland, encircled the colonial-style house, with a wooden veranda, a balcony and a brick-and-board façade. Although not in harmony with anything else in the area, the house was breathtakingly beautiful, with the warm russet bricks giving way to the pale green-tinged boards, and the slate roof glinting in the winter sun, and although I'd never been particularly interested in property, I couldn't wait to look inside.

Bearing out Jess's affirmed interest in interior design, the inside of the house was like something from *Homes and Gardens*, with subtle colours and design features that demonstrated impeccable taste. However, beautiful as it was, I couldn't help feeling a certain coldness, with nothing out of place and no sign that anyone actually lived there.

Jess led me through the hall, where the ceiling went right up to the partially glazed roof and the sun made patterns on the floor, through to the kitchen at the back of the house. Here in this large airy space I finally had a sense of homeliness, despite its generous proportions. In comparison with what I'd seen of the rest of the house, this room had some "clutter": recipes and notes pinned on to a cork board on the wall, rubber boots on the mat by the patio doors, randomly scattered cushions on the window seat and a selection of utensils, knick-knacks on the surfaces and a couple of newspapers and an open book on the centre table. Someone definitely lived in this room, and I suspected Jess spent quite a lot of time here. This was borne out when Jess started to prepare a lunch of homemade soup and bread, while I started to fill her in on the sanitised version of my own life.

I told her about Tom and even about being raped, but pretended that my assailant was unknown to me and was never identified. I didn't really want to tell her anything about this, but realised that Tom would be hard to explain, and the dead husband story wouldn't work with someone who knew my age and the timing so well. This was something I had always managed to evade with Tom, by avoiding any reference to my age and hoping he wouldn't ask too many questions. I needed Jess to understand the importance of Tom not finding out the truth, and so told her the story that he'd grown up with. I explained how my parents had reacted to my predicament and their subsequent treatment of me when I refused to give Tom up, and told her this was why I had stayed away so long. I gave the reasons why I had decided to come back now, and how much planning had gone into hiding my identity so no-one would know who I was. I tried to keep as near to the truth as possible, as I hated lying to her, but how could I tell her it was her own father who had raped me? I hadn't realised that I had been relating this story to her with my eyes on the stone floor, subconsciously studying the texture and shades of each one; but when I finished my story and looked up to Jess's face, I was amazed to find her crying.

I was surprised. Even though we'd been very close as children, I didn't think what happened to me would have such an effect on her; but when she started to speak and her story slowly unfolded, it left me reeling with shock.

"In some ways I am luckier than you, Rachel, for I have a husband who I love more than anything else in the world. The only thing wrong with my life is that Colin and I will never have children, and I do envy you your lovely son."

Jess's revelation explained the feeling of sadness and lack that I'd sensed in her earlier. So I ventured to ask what the problem was, hopeful that perhaps it wasn't as final as she seemed to believe. However, her explanation of the reason for their childlessness came as a total shock.

"I cannot have children because I cannot make love," she said simply. "We have been married for ten years and in all that time I have never let Colin touch me."

I didn't know what to say, and just managed to stop my mouth from dropping open. Although we'd been close as children, this degree of intimacy was completely new territory and not something I had ever experienced with any friend before. I found it hard to imagine why Jess was telling me these personal details about her life, but then realised that, like me, without a mother, sister or even a close friend to discuss things with, she'd bottled it up for so long. I had no experience of marriage or sex, except for something that I preferred to forget, and so felt helpless in the face of this obviously serious problem, and had no way of advising her and nothing of comfort to offer. However, I couldn't help feeling it must be this Colin's fault; after all, who could fail to love and cherish Jess?

Seemingly oblivious to my silence, Jess continued, "Colin is so good to me and swears that he doesn't mind, but I know that he can't be happy and I'm sure he's had many opportunities to find satisfaction elsewhere, but I truly don't think he ever has."

This left me very confused and certainly not able to lay the blame at his door. Fishing around in the depths of my mind, I came up with something about possible counselling or some kind of therapy, but was taken aback to hear Jess say that they had tried both, but she'd been unable to continue when they started to delve into the reasons behind her problem.

"How do you tell someone that your own father abused and raped you repeatedly for over nine years," she said.

I felt the breath leave my body, just as surely as if I had been kicked. Feelings of nausea and dizziness washed over me and, unable to breathe, I gripped the sides of my chair for fear of passing out. As the colour drained from my face, Jess completely misread the situation.

"You see," she said, "even you, who knew me so well, are disgusted when you know my terrible secret, so how could I tell a stranger? I do not know why he did those things to me when he should have loved and cared for me, but he always said it was because I wanted him to, and it's all so long ago now I don't remember. I didn't think I did, but he always said he was only trying to please me, so I must have done something to make him think I liked it, although I'm sure I didn't mean to, and I really hated it."

I felt the tears well up and all I wanted to do was reach out and hug her.

"Oh, Jess, my poor Jess, of course you didn't mean to. You did nothing wrong — you were a child, and he was the man you loved and trusted; that doesn't make you wrong or disgusting, it makes you normal — it's him that's disgusting!"

Jess lifted her head and looked me full in the face, as if trying to see if I was telling the truth or just fobbing her off. She'd carried her burden of guilt for so long — far longer than me, as her abuse had begun when she was just five years old, and her mother was still alive. In almost a whisper, she went on to tell me that she vaguely remembered trying to tell her mother what was happening when she was about eight years old, and then hearing a tremendous argument between her parents that night. She remembered that this was the day before her mother died in a car crash, so she never spoke to her again. At this point, she started to sob uncontrollably, and although I tried to comfort her, thinking it was just the memory of losing her mother, worse was to come as, between heart-rending sobs, she whispered, "He told me that Mummy died because I'd told her bad things, and that made me bad. He said it was my fault when all he'd ever done was loved me, and now we'd lost Mummy I would have to take care of him. From then on I had to sleep in his bed with him every night and keep him company."

I went from feeling so sorry for Jess to a venomous feeling of outrage, and with the feeling of fury inside me, the guilt that I'd harboured so long dropped away and left me feeling elated and free, but very angry.

I made an instant decision and told Jess the truth about Tom and his conception, and suddenly it was as if someone had opened a window and let the sun shine on both of us. As we clung to each other, weeping, a vision of John's butterfly came into my mind and I suddenly understood what he meant. Although the trauma of the past hour had drained us both, we'd come through it, gaining strength from each other and losing our own guilt in the knowledge of the other's suffering.

Despite the feeling of euphoria, something was still niggling at the back of my mind; it was something Jess had said that set alarm bells in my head, but I didn't know what, and it left me with a feeling of unease that I couldn't explain. I asked Jess if she'd ever reported her father to the police, but understood completely why her fear of people knowing had prevented her, even to this day. She, like me, had decided to get on with her life and pretend it had never happened, and once she'd persuaded her father to let her go to boarding school, which had been surprisingly easy, it never happened again. Jess told me she kept in touch with Richard, paying courtesy visits for birthdays and Christmas, and even going so far as to send a wordless card with an anonymous picture on the front and just signed Jess and Colin on Father's Day. Colin had no idea about Richard, but he'd taken an instant dislike to him when they first met, and so was happy to keep the contact to a minimum. This seemed to suit all of them and avoided embarrassment, and it certainly seemed as if Richard wanted nothing to do with her since she'd grown up and got married.

I was no longer worried about Jess spilling the beans to Tom, for she, more than anyone, understood the need for secrecy. For the first time in my life, I had found someone I could talk to about what had happened to me, and who didn't just understand how I had felt for so many years, but shared the same burden, and I really hoped I could do the same for her. When the time came to go home, I felt like we'd never been separated, and as we'd reminisced over selective memories on the way home, we descended into giggles and all the years fell away. After the emotion of the afternoon, it had been good to lighten the mood and indulge in nostalgia. We'd agreed that our confessions would remain between ourselves and not take over our lives, so the plan was to move on as the friends we'd always been, while always being careful to protect my identity. Although Jess expressed a desire to meet her "half-brother", it would be purely as a friend of his mother, and that had started us giggling again as Jess asked if this made me her step-mother. Although our mirth was somewhat out of place, the relief that laughter brought to the tension of the afternoon made us a little hysterical.

Although we'd swapped telephone numbers, we didn't make any arrangements to meet again, as we both knew that this was unnecessary. With the return of our easy friendship came the certainty that we would spend a lot of time together, and when she finally dropped me off at my cottage gate, we were once again as close as we'd ever been.

Chapter 8
AWAKENING

When I walked in the back door, Fern greeted me with a little of her own hysteria. She wasn't used to spending quite so long on her own and had consoled herself by demolishing a box of tissues all over the kitchen floor. In my present mood of euphoria, I had no heart for reprisals, and in between Fern's attempts at frantic greetings, I set about clearing up the mounds of "confetti" on the kitchen floor. I was amused to see that Fern couldn't hide her guilt, as there were tiny pieces of tissue stuck to her tongue as she tried to lick my hands.

I'd only just finished the clearing-up when Tom walked in. He seemed much happier than of late, but I knew that Richard was due to be in London all that day, so assumed that this was the reason for his good mood. As I looked at my tall, strapping son, I felt a surge of pride, but also a feeling of contentment, knowing that our move had been the right thing for him. He was happier here than he'd ever been in Essex, and in such a short time had seemed to grow from boy to man. I realised that this job wasn't going to be a lifetime career for him, but it was giving him an independence and time to make up his mind about the direction of his life, and

I had no doubt that gardens and growing things, which obviously gave him so much pleasure, would be a part of it.

Bringing myself back from my reverie, I asked him what he fancied for tea, but he said he wasn't very hungry and would be going out in a little while anyway. This was a bit of a surprise as, other than walking Fern or messing about in the garden, Tom hadn't done anything in the evenings since we'd arrived in the village. In fact, I'd been a bit worried that he hadn't made any friends and wouldn't settle. After the trouble in Essex, I was relieved he hadn't attached himself to the wrong crowd, but I would have liked him to make some friends and become part of some crowd. Trying not to sound as curious as I felt, I casually asked where he was off to, and was astonished to note the colour rush up from his neck, and the confusion in his reply as he tried desperately to sound as casual as me.

"I'm just going to the pictures with Beverley, and then we will probably come back here and meet some of her friends in the Buck for a game of darts."

I couldn't have been more pleased. He was making friends, and Beverley had seemed really nice the few times she'd been into the shop. I probably had a silly smile on my face, but Tom soon wiped that off with his attempt at bravado.

"Anyway, enough about me; how's your love life?"

It was my turn to colour up, although I replied without hesitation.

"What love life?" I said with an attempt at nonchalance, even though my stomach was turning somersaults; but Tom continued with some sarcasm.

"So what are you and John then — just good friends?"

"Don't be ridiculous," I said somewhat sharper than I intended. "Of course we are," then added in exasperation, "I'm almost old enough to be his mother."

"But not quite!" said Tom with a smile as he left the room.

When Tom left for his date smelling strongly of aftershave, the evening stretched before me long and lonely. I considered ringing Jess, but then thought her husband might answer the phone and have no idea of who I was, which would be difficult to explain.

I made myself a quick meal of cheese on toast with a cup of coffee, and when this was finished and cleared away, I noticed it was drizzly and cold outside, so decided to settle down with a book. However, Fern had other ideas, and after walking up and down, sitting down with huge sighs and jumping up at every little sound, I got the message and resigned myself to braving the rain and taking her out. Once outside, togged up in mac and boots, I was actually glad I had made the effort. The air was lovely and fresh and the dampness brought out the smell of grass and leaves as I walked. Fern had by now become so trustworthy that I was happy to let her run ahead, as she'd taught herself to jump on the verge and wait when a car came along, leaving me to walk with my hood up and hands in my pockets in a world of my own.

Fern jumped on the verge before I heard the approaching vehicle, and only when it drew up alongside was I suddenly aware of looking into the face of Richard — older, more lined and a bit greyer, but unmistakably Richard! Seized by an uncontrollable panic, my hand flew up towards my mouth in an involuntary movement that I managed to control before it reached my face, and it settled on my neck, just under my chin.

"Can I give you a lift anywhere?" he said in that horribly familiar upper-class drawl, but without any sign of recognition. "I'm going to the end of the village and you will be soaked if you stay out in this."

"No," I snapped, and then with a determined effort to compose myself, I added, "Thank you, but I like walking and I do not mind being wet" — and without waiting for a reply, I called to Fern and almost broke into a run as I hurried off down the road in front of the car. Richard overtook very slowly and I could almost feel his eyes on my back as he passed; but then he sped on his way and, as I let out a long sigh, I realised I had been holding my breath. The feeling of nausea that washed over me made me stop and lean against a telegraph pole, fully expecting to be sick; but it passed, and after a couple of deep breaths I was able to continue. If the shock hadn't been so great, I might have laughed at Fern's puzzled expression as she waited perfectly still and looking up at me with quiet concern.

Was there to be no end to this nightmare? It seemed that every time I took a step into the light, something or someone pushed me back into the dark hole of despair that I thought I'd left behind. As I struggled to pull myself back from wallowing in self-pity, and regain some composure, Jess came into my mind, and fear turned to seething anger. Before I'd had time to think it through, I was marching down the road towards the big house, fired by a grim determination and red-hot fury. I would kill him with my bare hands if I could; but I had no idea what I would do as I stomped determinedly towards his house. When Fern jumped on the verge again, I didn't even notice, and proceeded on down the road, oblivious of the car that was pulling up beside me.

"Where's the fire?" said a familiar voice, and John was beside me with his easy smile and friendly manner, which seemed totally at odds with the turmoil inside me. When I turned to face him, I was unaware of the tears running down my face. He took one look at me and was out of the car in an instant, wrapping me in his arms, and I just let him. I didn't care if we were seen, I didn't care about anything; I just felt warm and safe, which was exactly what I needed, so I clung on to him as if I was drowning.

Suddenly, he took charge. Helping me to the front of the car, he whistled to Fern and loaded her in the back. Without a word, he started the car and headed out of the village and up to the heath, where he pulled off the road and parked.

"Now," he said, "are you going to tell me what has happened, or do I have to find out?"

For the second time that day I started to talk, shakily at first, but then with more confidence as the floodgates opened and I told him everything, right from the beginning, without anger or emotion. Once I had started, I couldn't stop, but it was as if I was relating someone else's story. I missed nothing out, almost trying to shock him, in the certain belief that my revelations would drive him away. John listened without comment or interruption, but cold, grim anger had replaced his usual open, friendly countenance, and there was no doubt that I had indeed shocked him. However, he didn't turn away; he leaned across and took me into his arms, holding me so tenderly that I felt safer and more secure than I'd ever felt in my life. We stayed like this for what seemed like ages, not speaking, hardly daring to breathe. When John finally spoke, he was so quiet that I struggled to make out what he was saying, but there was no doubt of the venom in his words.

"The bastard! He can't be allowed to get away with what he's done to you and Jess and just carry on with his life as if he's done nothing wrong. I'll make bloody sure he knows exactly what he's done and he gets what he deserves."

The coldness in his voice and the hostile look on his face frightened me, and I was terrified of what he might do, but didn't know how I could stop him. In a state of panic, I begged him not to do anything which would give away our secret and hurt Tom. I could see him thinking, and then, in a calm but cold voice, he made me a promise: "I won't do anything that would hurt you, Jess or Tom; but one day, somehow, I'll get him!"

With no more said, he started the engine and pulled off the heath. I sat silently beside him, feeling very unsure of myself in his company. Gone was the comfortable companionship, and gone, too, was the stirrings of passion, replaced by a feeling of my own embarrassment and unworthiness. When we arrived at the cottage door, I glanced at my watch and was surprised at how early it was. It felt like hours had passed since I had left for my walk with Fern and I felt an overwhelming tiredness, brought about by the day's outpouring of emotion, and I knew things would never be the same again. I said a hurried goodbye and thank you to John and climbed out of the car. I was heading for the door when I heard him speak.

"Haven't you forgotten someone?"

I turned to see him letting Fern out of the back of his car. As she bounded up the path, I was surprised to see John follow.

"Isn't it about time you invited me in for coffee?" he said.

Unsure what to do or say, and not really wanting to be on my own, I just let him follow me into the cottage.

As soon as I'd closed the door, I went instinctively to the kettle and was struck by the humour of the situation. My world was falling apart. I was either on the verge of a forbidden love affair or I'd blown it completely and was destined to end my life as a lonely old woman; the way forward seemed fraught with danger, and here I was making a cup of tea! When I glanced at John it was as if he had read my mind, as he wore a look of mild amusement, and as I caught his eye he came forward, gently took my hand and led me to the stairs. I didn't resist; my chest had become tight and my breathing shallow, but I had no fear or revulsion for this man, just an overwhelming desire that I could no longer fight.

John had a natural sensuality which belied his youth, and the wisdom to take things slowly, which allayed any fear in me and allowed me to relax and enjoy the way he tenderly caressed my body. My one and only sexual experience had been rough and painful, and I was surprised to find that the softness of his touch brought out eroticism deep within me that I didn't know I possessed. As John slowly and gently removed my clothes, I was consumed with a desire to run my hands over his hard, young body, and as I lay exposed before him, I reached up to unbutton his shirt. Revelling in the warmth of his flesh beneath my hands, I slid them down and unzipped his jeans. Almost immediately, desire overtook us both and the slow and gentle approach gave way to fevered longing, as we touched and held and stroked each other. Our kisses became more intense and our breathing laboured, and as John's hands and fingers explored my body, I moaned with pleasure. When I could no longer bear it and wanted to scream with the intensity of my feelings, I pulled him on top of me and felt the hardness of him enter and thrust into me, driving me to a height of passion beyond anything I had ever known before, and then the world exploded into total ecstasy.

It was some time before we returned to reality, and as we lay sleepily in each other's arms, I felt total contentment, and all the bad things just melted away. Suddenly, Tom came into my mind and I jumped as if I was a naughty schoolgirl caught behind the bike sheds. John, once again reading my mind, said, "Don't worry, it's only 9.30, the film won't have finished yet."

Nevertheless, the mood was broken, and I began hunting for my discarded clothes, which seemed to be scattered randomly around the room, much to John's amusement. When we were both dressed, we went downstairs and, glancing over my shoulder at John with a half-smile, I returned to putting the kettle on.

"I'm sorry there's nothing stronger," I said, feeling that I should be bringing out wine in these circumstances, although, of course, I'd never been in these circumstances.

"Coffee's fine. I'm high enough already without any need for alcohol."

For the next hour we sat drinking coffee in virtual silence, each trying to come to terms with our feelings. Somehow I knew, that we were committed to each other, and however incongruous a couple we may be, I was sure that we belonged together. Gone were all my initial doubts, and although we'd not spoken, I knew that John felt the same way; there was just this companionable feeling of contentment that made it all seem right. Fern obviously agreed with me, as she'd carefully positioned herself on the floor across John's feet but with her head on mine, as if to join us together. I didn't think Tom would be so easy to win over and was very worried about what he would think; after all, John was barely three years older than him, and this new relationship was bound to raise difficult questions about my own age. With a feeling of utter elation, I realised that for the first time in my life I could talk about my worries to someone else, and so I broached the subject of Tom. With the assurance of youth, John said that Tom would get used to the idea, but he did think I should tell him the truth about my age, and just let him conclude he'd been conceived before I'd married his father. I thought this would prompt too many questions and lead to even more lies, but I had to agree that it was probably the only way to avoid hurting him. However, I would choose my moment, and now wasn't the time. Conscious of the fact that he would soon be arriving home, I thought it best not to confront him with the situation, and so, reluctantly, I asked John to go. He made no protest, but as he got up to leave, he once again took me into his arms and kissed me tenderly — and Tom chose that moment to burst through the door! It was difficult to know who was the most embarrassed, but Tom was the first to recover.

"Hi, you two," he said, as if nothing had happened, and he seemed in a very buoyant mood. "Is there anything to eat? I'm starving."

We hurriedly said our goodbyes in a very formal manner and then I joined Tom in the kitchen.

"I know what you must be thinking," I said. "I know he is much too young for me, but I'm not as old as you think, you know." Aware of the colour flooding my face and a tendency to gabble, I shut up and waited for the inevitable questions and ultimate disapproval.

"Don't be silly! I know exactly how old you are — Granny told me — and what's age got to do with anything anyway?"

To say I was stunned would be an understatement, and I was suddenly aware that my mouth was gaping open and closed it quickly.

"What else did Granny tell you?" I asked, and he went on to tell me that before she died Granny Wilson had thought that Tom should know the truth about his birth, at least as much as she knew. She told Tom that his mother had got pregnant at thirteen by a boy who didn't stand by her, and had made up the story about his father to avoid all the questions. Tom told me that at the time he'd been very angry, especially with me, and that's why he'd got into so much trouble. He thought this proved that I didn't really want him and he was nothing but an inconvenience to me, and obviously of no interest to his father, whoever he was. "I just wanted to fit in somewhere," he told me. "And that's why I tried to impress the crowd I got in with; but since we came here, I've had time to think."

"Is that a good thing?" I hardly dared ask.

"Well, yes, I think so. I realised why you did what you did, and also that it was much better for me at school having a dead father rather than none at all."

"Well, that's something I did right, then."

"Yeah, and, well, I suppose you didn't have to keep me; you could have given me up and carried on with your life, so I sort of understood, although it took me a while."

"Well, I'm glad it's out in the open, but I want you to know that although before you came along, I planned to have you adopted, the minute I set eyes on you I couldn't let you go."

"Even so, it would have been much easier to let me go, and I understand now how difficult it must have been for you to keep me when you were so young yourself. When I started to think about it, I realised how hard you had to work to keep me, so I sort of got over my hang-ups and decided that I don't want to know who my Dad is. I don't need him, but I am very proud of my Mum."

I was completely taken aback by his maturity and his apparent lack of concern over John, and I was so relieved not to have the scene I'd envisaged. Then, in a flash of inspiration, or perhaps Mother's intuition, I suddenly realised why Tom was in such a good mood.

"How did your date go?" I asked, and noticed the broad smile that lit up his face.

"Fine," he said. "We had a great time."

I couldn't help thinking this was an understatement, and my heart warmed to Beverley. As Tom busied himself cutting bread for toast, I suddenly realised how hungry I was, and so we finished an eventful evening munching toast and drinking cocoa in companionable silence, both deep in our own thoughts.

Chapter 9
REVELATIONS

I slept very heavily that night; exhaustion, brought about by the day's emotional turmoil, took its toll and resulted in weird dreams where Richard chased me along dark lanes in his car, John and Tom called me in different directions, and Jess waited in a lay-by, revving her engine and preparing for a head-on collision. When I woke in the early hours, I was aware of a feeling of unease about something that I just couldn't fathom. My thoughts turned to John and, although this brought its own worries, I knew he wasn't the problem nagging at the corner of my mind; and remembering how well Tom had taken the situation, I knew it wasn't him, either. I recognised the feeling as the same as I had felt at Jess's, and I knew it was something that she'd said which triggered a childhood memory that I couldn't put my finger on. I pushed it to the back of my mind, remembering that I had far more pressing matters to think about; but there it remained, niggling and nagging, and I knew I would have to come back to it.

There seemed little point in staying in bed now as I was fully awake, so I decided to go down and have a cup of coffee. I was filled with a feeling of elation and realised I was smiling to myself as I made the coffee. Thinking back to the previous evening, I couldn't help but be surprised by my own sensuality and wondered why I didn't feel the revulsion that had almost been part of my DNA since the attack all those years ago. It was clear by what Jess had told me that her abuse had had a profound effect on her ability to enjoy sex, so why was it that I was able to overcome it and experience such deep and true pleasure. Perhaps it was because for me it was just the one attack, and traumatic though that was, it was just one event in my life and I was able to get away from it, whereas for poor Jess it went on for years with no escape.

There was now no doubt in my mind that I was in love, although it was curious how I knew this, as I had never experienced it before. I knew that I may well face disapproval and even ridicule for the age difference, and felt sure that I would be the one disapproved of, but although he was so much younger than me, John wasn't a child, so I could hardly be described as a cradle-snatcher! After the previous night, the thought of a life without him in it was unimaginable, and so I would have to brave my critics, whoever they may be. I was relieved and happy that Tom appeared not to be one of them, and seemed to accept the situation, as I couldn't have coped with him turning against me. However, I think this was partly due to an understanding borne of his own new relationship, and I was grateful for that.

I had just made the coffee when Tom appeared tousle-headed at the foot of the stairs, reminding me of the little boy who used to come down at his Gran's house because there were goblins in his bedroom. After making himself a cup of coffee, he joined me at the table and caught my eye. Seeing the humour of the situation, we both giggled like a couple of naughty kids.

"It must be love," I said, and although Tom suppressed a laugh, he didn't disagree.

While we sat drinking our coffee and making small talk, I couldn't help noticing how often Beverley's name featured in the conversation. "Beverley says" and "Beverley thinks" preceded most of Tom's comments, and I was amused by his obvious need to include her in all his thoughts. However, a rather more worrying aspect of their conversation concerned Beverley's young sister Lynda. It seemed that since their Mum died Beverley had more or less brought Lynda up, and since she'd been working for Richard, she'd often taken her with her to work. Lynda, who was twelve, had a passion for drawing and was very good at it, so it wasn't difficult to keep her amused while Beverley was working, and she would often leave her sitting at the kitchen table with sketchbook and pencils whilst she cleaned the rest of the house. Tom was now telling me that on these occasions Richard often sat and watched her and seemed genuinely interested in what she was doing. He found this strange as Richard hardly spoke to him or Beverley, but it seemed Lynda was the apple of his eye.

I heard the alarm bells in my head almost as soon as he started telling me, but didn't know what to say. I could hardly tell Tom that Richard couldn't be trusted with young girls, but I knew I must do or say something to protect Lynda.

"She should get outside more," was all I could think of. "It's not good to stay cooped up indoors; can't you take her out in the garden with you?"

Tom looked puzzled by this response, and pointed out that when he was young, they didn't even have a garden. I knew I wasn't making much sense, and my feeble attempt to protect Lynda was useless, but unsure of what else to do, I dropped the subject to give me time to think. However, I knew I would have to come back to it, and this was yet another thing gnawing at the back of my mind.

For the next few months, life was relatively uneventful. John and I settled into a relaxed and loving relationship, which defied all the laws of probability, and it became stronger despite the age gap. I spent quite a lot of time with Jess, who had become a regular visitor to the cottage, and a familiar figure to Tom; but although I'd met Colin once or twice, I didn't see much of him, as when he wasn't working, he and Jess spent all their time together, seemingly content with each other's company. A few weeks after our first meeting, Jess once again confided in me, telling me that she and Colin had become much closer. Although not yet ready for full intercourse, she was able to be far more intimate with Colin and was really enjoying it. She put this down to our talk and explained that finding out about my own abuse had somehow made her feel far more able to accept her own abuse as just that and not in any way her fault, and this had a positive effect on her feelings of unworthiness. Colin had noticed the difference in her, and in his gentle and loving way had managed to make her feel loved and cherished without putting any pressure on her. After so many years of feeling dirty and degraded, she was beginning to realise that she'd been a victim and was now free. This new freedom gave her a sparkle that not only boosted her own confidence, but also delighted Colin, and they were behaving like a courting couple. Jess told me that she had feelings of desire that she'd never expected to feel, and the only reason she held back was her fear of how she would react if things went further. She was worried that she might freeze if things became too intimate, and didn't want to hurt Colin by leading him on, only to turn him away at the last moment. I felt I had to tell her about my own experience with John, and without going into details assured her that no memories encroached on our passion, which had only increased with familiarity. The loving and caring relationship I shared with John had no similarity to the rape, and my feelings for him and the intensity of our lovemaking was a world away from Richard and his perverted lust. Although her abuse had lasted so much longer, I was sure that now she'd felt the first stirrings of passion, she would overcome all her fears if she would only talk to Colin and tell him the truth. Jess said she was so frightened that this might turn him away from her that she dared not risk it, but deep down I think we both knew that one day she would talk to him about it. I hadn't told her of my fears for Lynda and decided not to, concerned that it might stir up old memories and make things more difficult for her and Colin.

We rarely talked of Richard at all, and as Jess paid only courtesy visits, and I avoided him altogether, there wasn't any need for him to feature in our gossip. However, one day his name did crop up, as Jess had noticed him standing by his car on the side of the lane looking helpless, when she was on the way over to see me. She'd felt obliged to stop and ask what was wrong, only to find that he was waiting for the AA to come and change his wheel. Jess wasn't surprised, as she told me that although Richard's father, her grandfather, had been a mechanic and had insisted that he learned about cars from an early age, he'd been determined not to go into the family garage business. He considered this type of work beneath him and had turned his back on his training, refusing even to check the oil and water on his own car, preferring to pay someone else to get their hands dirty, as he put it.

Although Jess had a trolley jack in the back of her car, and was quite capable of changing the wheel herself, she decided not to offer, and, refusing to feel guilty, let him wait for the AA to come the fifteen miles or so from the nearest town. I wasn't listening, for as soon as Jess had said that Richard wouldn't touch the car, a memory had flashed into my mind. I was a small girl playing hide and seek with Jess, and as I ran in the garage to see if she was there, I saw Richard standing next to his wife's car. There was a spanner in his hand and he was covered in grease, and I could now clearly remember the look of surprise and what I now recognised as guilt when he saw me.

"Just mending the car," he said, and I accepted this as quite normal, for my own father often tinkered with our ancient old banger; but now I realised it wasn't normal — it was at best suspicious and at worst positively sinister, for the next day Jess's Mum had died in that very car! I didn't want these thoughts or memories and tried to banish them, but as I sat wrestling with this unbidden revelation, Jess caught sight of my face.

"Whatever is wrong, Rachel?" she said. "You look as though you've seen a ghost."

I didn't know what to say; even though it was such a long time ago, I knew that Jess still felt the loss of her mother, and her father's words about it being her fault still haunted her. Deciding that the truth was better than deception, and there had already been more than enough of that, I told Jess what I'd remembered.

At first, I could almost see Jess battling with her mixed feelings and not wanting to believe what I was telling her. I realised that if my suspicions turned out to be true, she would be the loser. If Richard had tampered with her mother's car, it could only be because of what Jess had told her about her father, and therefore the blame would still be hers. She said as much to me, but I refused to let her go down this route. "Sometimes, Jess, I almost think you like feeling guilty — of course it wasn't your fault, any more than the abuse was. Richard is responsible for his own sick behaviour, and if he did mean to do away with your Mum, it could only mean one thing — she believed you and she was going to protect you, so you owe it to her to believe in yourself."

This tirade shocked Jess, but she had to admit that I was probably right, and she sat in stunned silence for some time before saying, "So now I'm the child of a murderer as well as a pervert," and a little voice inside me was saying, "And so is Tom."

Jess went on quietly, "I know he raped you and how he ruined your life, but at least you are not his daughter, and you do not have to face having a murderer for a father."

I felt as if I suddenly carried the weight of the world on my shoulders. "No," I said, "but Tom is his son!"

Silence reigned; there wasn't anything more to say. We'd both reached the conclusion that our suspicions were probably justified, but there was little either of us could do about it, and, even if we could, we didn't dare drag up the past for fear of it ruining the future.

When Tom walked in from the kitchen, we were horrified. My stomach turned somersaults and my heart was banging in my chest — how long had he been there and how much had he heard? I searched his face, but couldn't see any sign of shock or distress. He said he'd only just come home and had come in via the back wall into the garden and spotted Jack Butler coming out after spraying the roses for him, which all sounded plausible. However, he did seem quiet for the rest of the evening, picked at his tea and went to bed early, which was very unusual.

I didn't see Jess again for several days and was a bit worried about her state of mind. She'd been very quiet when she left after Tom came home, and I knew she would be brooding over her newfound knowledge. However, I also had all my own worries about whether Tom had overheard anything and what to do if he had. As if I didn't have enough to worry about, John had finally persuaded me to have a go at competing at a trial with Fern, which was very scary. The upside was that getting ready for the trial required daily training sessions, so I saw a lot of John, and so I decided to put all my efforts into that and pushed my concerns to the back of my mind.

When Jess dropped in for a cup of tea about a week later, the change in her was dramatic. Far from the depressed and anxious person I was expecting to see, she was smiling and happy, and seemed to glow with an inner confidence and delight. It was obvious that something had happened to make her feel this good, and I couldn't wait for her to tell me what it was.

We took our tea into the garden, and as we sat down at the old rustic table, I just had to say something. "What, or should I say who, has put that smile on your face?"

Jess looked down, blushed and then giggled with embarrassment. She didn't need to say any more — I guessed the rest.

"So when did all this happen, and why?"

"I took your advice and told Colin everything, even about how we think Mum died. He was so angry that I thought he was going to walk out on me and go and kill my Dad. I was sure I'd made a terrible mistake telling him, but he suddenly calmed down and put his arms round me. He reacted much the same way as your John, swearing that he would find a way to get back at Dad; but his first concern was for me, and as he held me close and kissed my head, I clung to him as I never had before."

She broke off then and went very red, so I could guess the rest: his love and tenderness to her had awoken something deep inside, just as John had done to me, and the inevitable conclusion was the consummation of their long-standing barren marriage.

It seems that the outpouring of passion had opened the floodgates, and since their first hesitant beginnings, they had found they were highly compatible and were totally besotted with each other.

Without going into too great a detail, and still blushing furiously, Jess hinted that they were making up for lost time, and had hardly been apart for the last week. She told me they were planning a holiday in the sun as a sort of second honeymoon, even though the first had been a non-event. However, there was a cloud on the horizon: Richard's birthday was coming up, and Jess didn't know how she or Colin would handle it. Traditionally, they would go out for a meal and make polite conversation, while watching him open an expensive but impersonal gift over which he would feign delight. However, even this much was more than she could face with her new-found knowledge and recent happiness, and she was very afraid that Colin wouldn't cope and might do or say something they would both regret. The perfect solution was to try to get a last-minute booking for their holiday and put a card and gift in the post, so this is what she'd decided to do. Unfortunately, it wasn't proving easy, as Colin insisted he had something to sort out before they went, and although he didn't go into details, he said he couldn't go until it was done. He was hopeful that he would be ready in time, so on that basis Jess had decided to go ahead and book it anyway, and she was on her way into town to go to the travel agents and called to ask if I wanted to go with her.

As it was one of my free days and I wasn't due to meet John for training until the evening, I decided to go with her, and so we set off, full of high spirits, planning to shop and have lunch, and I couldn't help being reminded of the way we were as kids.

During the drive to town, Jess became thoughtful and suddenly asked, "Has Tom been okay? Do you think he did hear anything when he walked in on us?"

My heart sank and the jolly atmosphere of a few minutes ago deserted me.

"I don't think so. Although he's certainly been quieter than usual, and doesn't seem to want to chat like we used to when he gets home in the evenings. I'm sure if he'd heard anything, he would have asked questions by now; I don't think he would have kept it to himself. So maybe he's just having a bad time at work and that's getting him down."

"Yes, that's probably it," Jess said. "So let's forget all our worries and enjoy our day." This seemed like a good idea, although it was hard to regain the care-free feeling that had marked the start of our journey.

Somehow, we managed it and the day was a total success. Jess was able to book a flight to Corfu which left late afternoon on Richard's birthday, and in the light of this we'd a good excuse to go on a shopping spree for holiday clothes and sun cream. We enjoyed a long lunch at a riverside café, sitting under a parasol in the garden, and then spent the afternoon in exclusive shops trying on expensive clothes I certainly couldn't afford — a complete waste of time, but a great deal of fun!

When we arrived back at the cottage, we were amazed how late it was, and Jess rushed off home, excited about telling Colin her news. I felt a little pang of jealousy: I'd never been abroad and had never really thought about it before, but I couldn't help imagining hot sun, silver sand and John with a touch of envy. I very quickly put that thought out of my mind; even if I could afford to go on a romantic holiday with John, who would look after the cats, the dog and Tom?

I was genuinely delighted with Jess's newfound happiness; she deserved to be happy for the rest of her life after what she endured at the hands of her father, and perhaps now she would. My own abuse had been nothing in comparison to Jess's, and now, when I thought of Richard, my anger centred far more around the treatment of his daughter and possibly his wife than my own, which had been short-lived in comparison. Not so John, however, who couldn't even hear the man's name spoken without brooding upon his hatred and a means of retribution. This frightened me, and was the only difficulty between us, so I avoided any reference to him, although Tom sometimes mentioned him, but only to complain about his unreasonable behaviour and to tell us how much he hated him.

For some reason it seemed that Richard took great delight in making Tom's life a misery. He would find fault with everything he did, and ridicule him in front of Beverley, which was mortifying. Tom had been speaking to Jack Butler in the pub and had told him that, despite Richard's criticism, gardening was what he wanted to do. Jack had suggested that he found out what courses were on offer at the local Agricultural and Horticultural College, and he'd followed Jack's advice and made some enquiries. For the first time in ages, we had a real talk about it over tea one evening and he told me that he'd discovered that there was a two-year course on landscaping and garden design which sounded very interesting. Unfortunately, he needed to be eighteen to enrol, and felt he would have more chance if he gained some experience, so he was prepared to stick out the job until he was old enough, although he told me there were times when he thought of walking away.

When he told me some of the things Richard had said to him, I was fuming and was both amazed and impressed that he hadn't walked out before. It was ironic that I could remember Richard many years ago upsetting Jess by bemoaning the fact that he had no son, and now, unbeknown to him, he was faced with the son he longed for, but didn't seem to like what he saw. I admired Tom's determination to see it through and told him so. I was proud of his maturity in planning a worthwhile future for himself and was grateful for Jack's part in his decision to pursue the career he'd set his heart on. It did occur to me that money might be a bit tight, but I'd hardly touched my redundancy money, and could always go back to full-time work if necessary, so if he needed help, he could have it.

"Well, I think you've made the right decision, and if you can stick the job for another few months it'll give you experience and a bit a cash to get you started, which can't be bad," I said.

John came round that night so we could go out and do some training with Fern; the trial was only a week away now and I was beginning to get a bit nervous. I didn't think we were anywhere near ready, and it occurred to me that it was strange so much was happening on the same day. The trial was the day of Richard's birthday, and also the day that Jess was off on holiday. Earlier in the evening, Tom had said that Richard had given him that day off, although he didn't say why, but I guess he'd made plans for his birthday. With an unexpected weekend day off, Tom had decided to take the train down to Essex and visit some old school friends. This worked well for me, as it meant I could go off to the trial without feeling guilty about leaving Tom at a loose end all day fending for himself.

The evening's training went well and filled me with confidence. Fern was obviously pleased with herself as well, for at the end of the training walk she raced round in big circles, returning only to bark, jump up and then take off again. John and I laughed at her antics and I thought this might be a good moment to ask John for advice on the Lynda situation, which had been playing on my mind for days. I really didn't want to burden him with the problem, but even after days of thought I hadn't come up with any solutions and needed to talk it over with someone else to get another view on it. At the mention of Richard's name, John's expression changed immediately and I almost regretted bringing the subject up; but I gritted my teeth and carried on telling him of my concerns and, after a moment, he regained his composure and set about trying to sort out what I should do. The situation wasn't easy, as any sort of warning would need an explanation, and I wasn't in any position to offer one without giving away too much. John and I tried to think of ways of keeping Lynda away from Richard, but knew it would look very strange if we just started taking an interest in her out of the blue. Then John had an idea: he had been talking to his Mum about needing some part-time help at the boarding kennels. Tom had mentioned Lynda's great love of animals, and how she spent her time drawing dogs and naming the breeds, so he wondered if a job at the kennels could help them out and keep her out of Richard's way. I immediately felt better, sure that this would work, and was so glad I had talked to John. John said he'd mention it to his mother the next day, and if she agreed and Lynda was keen, they should be able to sort something out fairly quickly, without anyone being any the wiser.

The decision made, we regained our good humour, and so when John suggested a drink at the local, I thought "why not?" We'd hidden away for too long and if our relationship was ever going to last, we would have to face people and deal with their prejudices; so we loaded Fern into John's car and headed for the 'local'. Reactions when we entered the pub ranged from disinterest to welcoming smiles, although it was impossible not to be aware of some curious glances. However, when Jack Butler spotted us, he greeted us like old friends and everyone seemed to know John, so it was less of an ordeal than I'd feared, and within a short while we were chatting with the regulars, who seemed to accept us as a "couple". It was strange to hear them refer to "you and John" in conversation, and I had the feeling that word of our relationship had travelled before us, as it tended to do in small communities, and people had been aware of our situation almost as long as we had. It was good that there was no open animosity, and everyone seemed genuinely friendly. In the congenial company we stayed longer than we'd intended, and were amazed when the landlord called time. As we said goodbye to our companions and left the pub, I was aware of a feeling of "belonging" that was similar to how I'd felt all those years ago, in this very village, before my world fell apart, and for the first time since I'd moved back here, I felt like I'd come home. Somehow, John and even Jack were part of this feeling, and I knew that with John and Tom at my side and people like Jack and Jess as friends, this village really was my home and I would never again feel the crushing loneliness that had been so much part of my life since I'd left.

Chapter 10
RETRIBUTION

On the morning of the trial I woke early and suddenly remembered that this was Saturday and began to feel slightly sick — there was no going back to sleep. John had picked a local trial for Fern's first attempt, and with an eleven o'clock report time we wouldn't need to leave much before ten. I was far too nervous to stay in bed so, being careful not to wake Tom, I crept down the stairs with Fern padding quietly behind me, as if she, too, was aware of the need for silence. Once downstairs, however, Fern returned to her usual exuberant self and demanded to be let out, so I opened the back door and was met with a stream of sunlight. It was a comfort to know that it would at least be dry for our first outing. I'd had visions of torrential rain and gales, and Fern not hearing a word I was saying, so it was a relief to see the sun. However, I thought to myself, "Now there's no excuse," and then, pulling myself together, I remembered positive thinking, took a deep breath and set about getting ready. I made a cup of coffee and measured out Fern's breakfast, calling her in as I put down her bowl. Fern began tucking into her breakfast, completely unaware of the importance of the day, and I sat down at the kitchen table with my coffee and became lost in my own thoughts. Thinking about the trial naturally included John, and when my stomach tightened, I wasn't sure if it was the event or the man that was causing the excitement.

The conversation of the previous evening came unbidden into my mind, when, once again, our contentment had been shattered with the mention of Richard's name. John told me he'd spoken to his mother and it was all arranged that Lynda would work at the kennels on Saturdays and after school, starting the following Saturday, when he would be there to show her the ropes. Tom came home during this conversation and told us that for some reason Richard seemed annoyed about Lynda's new job and had told Beverley it would interfere with her schooling. He even said that if she needed to earn money, he would find her a job, although Tom said he'd no idea what he had in mind. Sadly, I did, and was relieved to hear that both Beverley and Lynda had stuck to their guns and it was good to know that with Beverley not working the following day, Lynda would have no need to go there again. I'd thought it was strange that Richard had given both Tom and Beverley the day off on his birthday and wondered what he had planned, but had then realised that I didn't care and immediately felt better.

I'd said to Tom that whatever Richard had planned for his birthday, it had the added bonus of giving him and Beverley the day off, although they didn't seem to be spending it together. The loathing in Tom's voice was surprising when he told me about the terrible day he'd had with Richard, making Beverley cry, and threatening to sack him, and said that he didn't care what he did on his birthday, and he could preferably drop down dead.

When I'd looked at John and seen the tension on his face and the way his hands were clenched, I'd feared he might reveal his anger, which would have been difficult to explain, so I'd quickly changed the subject, and asked him if he thought his collie bitch Meg was in pup. She'd been mated a couple of weeks previously and I knew he'd been watching her avidly to spot any early signs. I'd been relieved to see his expression change when he started to talk about his hopes for the forthcoming litter, and his tension turn to excited pride.

However, in the back of my mind was the sudden and worrying realisation that, for reasons of their own, Tom and John hated Richard almost as much as I did!

The sound of Tom stirring upstairs brought me back to the present time and the trial ahead, so I got up to flick the kettle back to life. It wasn't only me who had a big day in front of them, as Tom was going back to Essex to see some of his friends. It was also the day that Jess and Colin were flying out to Corfu, although they weren't leaving until almost lunchtime and I pictured Jess packing all the things we bought on that lovely day in town; so it seemed everyone was doing something exciting.

When Tom came down, he was still yawning and sleepy, and surprised to see how early it was.

"Is it really only six?" he said. "I thought it was much later. What are you doing up so early?"

I reminded him about the trial and suggested that he could go back to bed if he wanted; but, having made the effort to get up, he decided to have a cup of coffee and plonked himself down at the table next to me. I realised that he was expecting me to make it for him and didn't have the heart to make him get up and do it himself, so I went across to get him a mug out of the cupboard.

"What's Beverley doing with her day off?" I asked.

"I asked her if she wanted to come with me to Essex, but she doesn't know any of my friends and said she'd rather spend the day shopping — or at least, on Richard's wages, looking!"

When Tom talked of Beverley, he wore his heart on his sleeve, and seemed determined to make sure everyone else liked her. This wasn't difficult as far as I was concerned: she'd almost become part of the family since her Dad had started teaching Tom to drive, and while she waited at the cottage for them to finish the lessons, we'd sat and chatted and become really good friends. I liked her down-to-earth character, and although it was clear she was besotted with Tom, I was pleased to note she was no pushover. She had her own opinions, which was a good thing, as I knew Tom could be quite self-opinionated and stubborn, so it would do him good to have someone who wouldn't necessarily agree with everything he said.

It was nice for me to have another female to talk to, as Jess had been so engrossed in Colin and the holiday lately, I'd hardly seen anything of her. Possibly because of losing her mother at an early age, Beverley seemed far more mature than her years, so we got on really well, and the clincher as far as I was concerned was that Beverley adored Fern and the cats and they also liked her, which was good enough for me. I think perhaps she, too, enjoyed some female company, as other than her little sister she didn't have time for too many girlfriends, and with no mother to talk to I hoped that in some small way I filled the void.

Tom left to catch his train just before nine o'clock, by which time I'd packed a lunch, laid out my waterproofs and boots, and checked the schedule several times. It was still almost an hour before we were due to leave and I was at a loss to know what to do with myself. Eventually, I could bear the inactivity no longer and decided to take Fern for a quiet stroll around the village; nothing too strenuous before the trial, but a chance for both of us to stretch our legs before the journey, and for me to get control of my nerves. It was a beautiful morning and, although well into September, it felt more like Spring. Fern, with no reason to be excited, trotted happily along the lane beside me and I was glad I'd decided to come out. The early sun filtered through the hedge and gave Fern's black coat an amber glow, and the warm breeze would make for good scenting conditions at the trial, I told myself, although I was far too inexperienced to know if this was in fact true. As I walked, I felt my nerves evaporating as the world turned into a warm and friendly place where nothing could go wrong or disturb the perfection of the morning. I was jolted back to reality by a car speeding past and out of the village so suddenly that I didn't have time to tell Fern to get on the bank, but luckily, she did it anyway. It had all but gone before I realised that it was Colin's car, and wondered what he was doing in the village on the day he was flying off to Corfu. Then I remembered him telling Jess that he had things to do before he could leave, and she was worried that he wouldn't make the flight on time. Maybe that was why he was in the village and in such a hurry, and when I thought about it, I realised that, as an estate agent, he could have any number of reasons for being there. Then it occurred to me that Jess might have asked him to deliver their gift to Richard before they went, and although in the circumstances this seemed highly unlikely, he was coming from that direction and seemed in an awful hurry, so perhaps he'd just dropped off the present and left.

Well, that was the best I could come up with, and I glanced at my watch and realised that I'd been out a bit longer than intended, so, calling to Fern, I did a quick about-turn and hurried back the way I'd come. Although my leisurely stroll had turned into a bit of a hustle on the way back, there was no need, as we arrived back at the cottage with about fifteen minutes to spare before John was due to pick us up. I remembered to fill a drinking bottle for Fern and put it with her bowl in a bag near the door next to the other stuff, and then there was nothing to do but wait. When it got to ten past ten, I started to get a bit concerned, so rang the kennels. John's Mum said he had left about nine o'clock, which was odd, both because he'd left so early but also because he hadn't yet arrived, and as he only lived just outside the village, I couldn't think why it had taken him so long. Just then I heard his car pull up outside, so I told his mother he'd arrived and she wished me luck and said goodbye. When I opened the door, I was a bit taken aback to see John looking hot and bothered and with blood on his hand and his jeans.

"Whatever's happened?" I said.

"Well, I meant to arrive early as I guessed you'd be getting in a stew, but I got a puncture and I've been all this time trying to change the wheel. The bloody wheel nuts must have been welded on. I couldn't budge them at all and I've ripped my knuckles trying."

"Oh, what a pain. How did you manage it?"

"I eventually got some movement by jumping on the wheel brace, but I fell off a couple of times and now I'm a right mess."

"Is it okay now? Can we still go?"

"Yes, but look at the state of me."

He was sweating and dirty and obviously not in the best of moods, so I thought it best to drop the subject and just load up the car.

It had been a funny morning so far, with everyone rushing about and getting into a state apart from me, who was competing, and yet managed to enjoy quite a serene start to my day.

The journey to the trial was rather more fraught than expected with time getting short, and traffic heavy, but we arrived at the venue with five minutes to spare and I went straight to the base to report in. I had only entered the bottom class (or stake, as they are known in trials) and so there was no tracking test, so I just had to report to the judge for my search test when I was ready.

Although when I had met John, I'd no idea what working trials were about and had to admit that to begin with I was far more interested in the man than the sport, over the time that we had been training together I had really got hooked. There was so much to them, and although so far, I had only just scratched the surface of all the things we had to learn, I had a very good teacher and no lack of enthusiasm.

Working trials were evolved as a way of testing the character and ability of military and police dogs and thus were mostly aimed at the German Shepherd, or Alsatian as they were then known. The tests consisted of a series of exercises that these dogs would be called upon to carry out in their working lives, and so tracking and searching as well as general obedience were all part of the tests. In addition to this, dogs had to prove that they were agile by negotiating a series of obstacles, and in the top stake they also had to show they could defend their handler and deal with trouble when sent to do so. That was back at the turn of the century, and since then the idea had caught on with ordinary dog owners with other breeds, who could see the excitement of the sport and wanted to have a go. These amateurs soon proved themselves to be every bit as good as the professionals, and some of the other breeds such as Dobermans, Boxers, Labradors and my own breed of Border Collie started to populate the stakes and have great success. Nowadays, although some police officers still came to compete, the sport was mostly for people like myself who just wanted to give their working dog a job to do.

So this is where we are today, and although I was only a very small part of the very bottom stake, I was still a "trialist" and proud to be one.

Although it was all very informal, I guessed 'when I was ready' actually meant now, so I went to get Fern and head off to do my search square.

From a less than perfect start, the day got better and better, and although John seemed a bit quiet at the start and I wondered what was on his mind, he brightened up and took more interest when Fern found two of the three articles in the Search Square, giving us enough points to qualify for that section. She then went on to do far better than I had expected in her Control and Agility sections, with enough for an overall qualification, and a third place! By three o'clock it was all over and we waited at the base for the presentation, which didn't take place until about five, when all the work was completed. I was thrilled at our achievement, and John seemed as happy as I was. Some of the other handlers who knew him came up to say well done to me, and all were really friendly and complimentary about Fern, and I felt like I'd won the Olympic Gold rather than a third place in the bottom stake! It seemed ridiculous that a piece of paper with our names on it meant so much, but that is all we came for and I was thrilled.

The journey home was at a somewhat more leisurely pace than our arrival, and we reached the village at about six thirty to find it swarming with police. I was amazed and couldn't imagine what was going on. It was unusual to see one policeman on a bike in our village, but as we passed the welcome sign, we saw a police car leaving and then two more as we went through the street. Policemen were all over the place, knocking on doors, and a police dog van came past us heading up the hill. My first thought was that someone had gone missing, and I wondered if it was perhaps a child, or one of the numerous elderly residents who had become a little confused.

"My Dad will know what's going on. I'll drop you off and go ask him, and then I'll give you a ring," John said, as he turned into the lane and pulled up outside the cottage. It was then that I saw the police officer standing at my own front door and, as I leapt out of the car, he came down the path to meet me. I felt myself go cold and, gripped with a terrible fear that something awful had happened to Tom, I waited to hear the worst. However, what the young constable told me wasn't what I was dreading, but something I couldn't have imagined in my wildest dreams. Richard was dead! He'd been found dead by the local window cleaner on the floor by the open French windows of his house at about mid-day. He said they were making house-to-house enquiries to find out if anyone had seen anything or anyone suspicious in the village that day.

When we told him that we'd not been at home all day, and couldn't be much help, he left, and we went inside. Tom hadn't yet returned and the cottage seemed strangely empty and quiet and, as the shock sank in, we, too, were quiet. I suddenly realised with horror that the police didn't make house-to-house enquiries when a person died of natural causes, and it seemed more likely that unless he'd suddenly decided to end it all, which was hard to believe, someone had actually hated Richard enough to kill him. When I shared this with John, he seemed reluctant to accept it, and said it could still have been an accident; but I didn't think they'd go to all the trouble of making house-to-house enquiries or be interested in any strangers in the village if they thought it was an accident.

"Perhaps it was a bungled burglary," John said. "Living in that big house does smack of wealth, and we all thought he was away for the day, so perhaps the burglar did as well."

"Yes, that's true, but I wonder why he was at home. He told Jess he wouldn't be, and gave both Tom and Beverley the day off, which is strange in itself."

When I mentioned Jess, I realised that she probably didn't know anything about it and I wondered whether or not I should tell her. I could get in touch with her in an emergency, as she'd left me with contact details, but I wasn't sure if I should. It wasn't as if she was close to Richard, and she was heading for the holiday of a lifetime. I didn't want to spoil her holiday, and she was unlikely to mourn his passing too much; in fact, if she'd been at home instead of the other side of the world, I might have wondered if she'd killed him herself!

John said it was probably best to leave it to the police, as they would no doubt discover where she was eventually and cut her holiday short, so best to leave her in ignorance while they could.

Just then, the phone rang and it was Jess. Unfortunately for her, the police had found out their plans from Colin's office and managed to contact the airport just before take-off. When John realised who was on the phone, he guessed it wouldn't be a brief conversation and gestured that he would be on his way. I gave him a wave and then turned my attention to Jess, who had arrived back home in a state of shock and was waiting for the police to arrive. She didn't think they would be there long as she had nothing to tell them and hadn't been there. I realised that they hadn't expected to be at home, so wouldn't have shopped or planned for an evening meal, so I asked Jess if they'd like to come over for something to eat. She seemed glad to accept the offer, and said they would be with me as soon as the police had finished with them, although they would have to let them know where they were going in case of any developments.

They arrived about an hour later, by which time I'd managed to feed Fern and the cats and put some jacket potatoes in the oven, which would at least give us the basis of a meal. Jess was white-faced and quiet and Colin, seemingly in an effort to make up for Jess's silence, had a tendency to babble, which was quite unlike his normally quiet, affable nature. I found some ham and salad to go with the potatoes and we sat around the table with the meal and mugs of coffee.

"This day has gone from bad to worse," said Jess a little irritably. "It didn't start well, with Colin disappearing to Heaven knows where, making us late getting away."

To which Colin replied with an uncharacteristic show of impatience, "Well, you can talk, Jess. Where were you when I *did* arrive home? You had disappeared with no explanation and have still not told me where you were."

"I only dashed out to get a couple of things in case you were not back in time for us to shop at the airport, and I wasn't gone more than half an hour," she said defensively. "And anyway, if you hadn't gone out, I wouldn't have bothered."

Fearing that this might turn into an argument with them both so strung up, I tried to change the subject from their rather fraught preparation to the devastating news at the airport. "When did the police arrive?" I asked.

"We were only a few minutes from boarding," said Jess, "and I know it sounds bad, but I wished they had missed us!"

"They would have caught up with us in Corfu," said Colin.

"Yes, maybe so, but perhaps we would have had one day in the sun before they tracked us down, and I don't care if it does sound heartless," she said vehemently.

In an effort to lighten the mood, I started to tell them about my day, and then, realising how trivial it all must sound in the light of the day's events, my voice trailed off and Jess suddenly exploded.

"I'm glad!" she said. "And it's no good pretending I'm not. I know its wicked and I should feel some sadness, but I don't; I just feel a massive sense of relief that at last it's all over and I really am free" — and with that she burst into tears!

Colin immediately started to comfort her and then made a statement of his own that was so cold that it took me by surprise.

"He only got what he deserved. It was only a matter of time before someone was bound to do it."

It was not until after they left that it occurred to me how strange his comment was, considering that at this stage they had no idea how Richard had died, and there was no suggestion that anyone had actually "done it", as Colin put it.

Not long after they left, Tom arrived home and seemed stunned by the news. So much so, in fact, that he had difficulty remembering much of what he had done that day, and I gave up asking him when all I got were vague answers. He decided to go and see Beverley and so didn't even stop to eat before heading off for the evening. With Colin and Jess leaving so early, and Tom going out as well, I wished I'd arranged to see John, but as I curled up on the sofa, resigned to a lonely evening in, there was a tap on the door and he came in. I was delighted to see him and told him that he must have read my mind.

"Don't I always?" he replied. "I certainly try to do whatever you want or need me to, even when you don't know yourself what that may be," — and although he smiled as if joking, I couldn't help wondering what he meant.

However, when he joined me on the sofa his nearness wiped out all thoughts and questions, and the day faded away as I rested my head on his chest and closed my eyes.

By the time he bent to kiss me, desire had overtaken us both, and when John slipped his hand inside my blouse and touched my breast, I was consumed with a passion so strong all thoughts of the day were banished from my mind. I moaned with pleasure as we sank to the floor and rolled around on the carpet, discarding our clothes with total abandon. We made love until we were both exhausted; perhaps it was an attempt on both our parts to blot out the events of the day. Which in no way diminished our pleasure in each other, and any ghosts were well and truly laid to rest!

We'd no sooner regained control of ourselves and dressed when Tom walked in, and I was so relieved he hadn't arrived any sooner. Although I was fairly sure he knew of my relationship with John, I was careful not to force it on him and certainly didn't want him walking in on our lovemaking. I made a mental note to myself to be more careful and then turned my attention to the menfolk, and suggested a cup of coffee. They both followed me into the kitchen, and as they sat at the table with their mugs of coffee the inevitable topic of conversation was Richard. Tom said he and Beverley had been down to the pub and it seemed to be common knowledge that Richard had bled to death from some sort of wound, but he didn't know where this information had come from. John said that when he'd spoken to his father, he'd said much the same, but as this information hadn't been officially released, John hadn't said anything. However, if it was the talk of the local, it seemed that someone had said something! According to Tom there were any number of theories circulating, from drug-dealing assassination to serial-killing vagrants, but most people seemed to think it must have been a burglary that went wrong, as Richard did have quite a lot of valuable antiques and was known to keep substantial sums of money in the house.

I asked Tom how Beverley and her family had taken the news, and he said that although she was quite shocked, Beverley didn't feel any great sadness as he'd never been anything but rude and unkind to her; but apparently Lynda was quite disturbed, which surprised Beverley and her Dad. She was apparently in quite a state, and although not exactly sad, she'd taken the news very badly and appeared to be unable to believe that Richard really was dead. I thought that this was a natural reaction from a young girl forced to acknowledge the death of someone she knew well, and pointed out this may have brought back memories of losing her mother, and reminded Tom how difficult he'd been when Nan had died.

John said that the burglary theory seemed the most likely, and no doubt that's what the police thought, so they probably wouldn't hear much more about it unless they found the culprit, which in the circumstances might prove impossible. I couldn't help wondering why nobody seemed to consider the possibility of Richard's death being an accident; it was as if it was easier to believe that someone had killed him, which in itself was strange.

When he had finished his coffee, John got up to leave and, as I saw him to the door, I wished for the umpteenth time that he didn't have to go. Although I knew he was very young and probably far too young to think about settling down, all I wanted was to share my life with him — go to bed with him and wake up in the morning with him beside me. As he kissed me goodbye, he held me tight, and before he released me, he gave me a short squeeze and, as if once again he had read my mind, said, "One day I won't be leaving and we will climb those stairs together," and then he was gone.

As Tom and I headed up the stairs to bed, I remembered the bright sunny morning and all the promise it held. It seemed so long ago that I'd come down these stairs full of excitement, and so much had happened since then, that the trial had been pushed to the back of my mind. Now, in spite of everything, I remembered our triumph, and as Fern settled down on the floor at the bottom of the bed, I got down on the floor and gave her a hug and told her, "Well done, you're a very clever girl," and Fern's tail gently thumped the floor.

Chapter 11
SUSPICIONS

I slept fitfully. Dreams of Fern running away in the middle of the trial mingled with pictures of Richard lying dead and covered in blood by his open French windows. My mind confused this image with my own memories of lying in much the same position on the same carpet all those years ago, and in my dream, it was me that was dead. I awoke suddenly with sweat pouring off me, and wondered if I'd cried out; but as I lay quite still in the dark, I heard nothing from Tom's room, so assumed he was still asleep. Unfortunately, I wasn't, and now fully awake, a glance at the green luminous numbers on the bedside clock told me it was only 3am. After the early start of the day before, I was determined not to get up and tried desperately to empty my mind and get back to sleep. No matter how hard I tried to think of nothing, the more the thoughts intruded and, as I unwillingly trawled through the depths of my darkest fears, I suddenly and quite inexplicably realised that everyone who I cared about and was close to were not only involved in the day's happenings, but were quite possibly suspects! This realisation hit me like a bolt from the blue, and the more I tried to dismiss the suspicions the more persistent they became. They all had a motive, and if the local gossip was right and Richard was killed between 9 and 10am, they all had the opportunity — including me! Well, I knew I hadn't done it, and I had as much reason as anyone, so why would I think any of the others had? I went through the morning's events in my mind and remembered that Tom's train left at 9am, so thankfully that put him in the clear. Then I remembered Colin in the village at about the right time, and where on earth had Jess been? Then there was John. I really didn't want to think about that possibility. He'd certainly been "missing" for the best part of an hour, and when he arrived his dishevelled and bloodied state, coupled with his unusually bad mood, was a bit suspicious; and then there was his comment about doing what I wanted, even if I didn't know what that was. What did that mean? I was horrified by my own thoughts and, realising that there was no chance of going back to sleep now, I got up and headed for the door.

Fern was surprised; not used to getting up in the middle of the night, but willing to join me in whatever I was doing, she followed me downstairs.

As I wandered aimlessly across to the kettle, I realised, not for the first time, how a hot drink could seem like the answer to all the world's problems, and the thought made me smile and brought back fond memories of Nan. After a feast of cocoa and chocolate biscuits, shared with Fern, I felt much more positive and decided to give sleep another go. The hot drink had obviously done its job, for when I got back under the covers, I fell asleep almost immediately and slept soundly without dreams until I was awoken by Tom going downstairs and Fern pacing up and down.

I hurried downstairs feeling guilty for having slept so late, to find Tom reading the Sunday paper, which had just arrived, and the headline "Suspicious Death in Small Village" jumped out from the front page. Even seeing it in black and white over Tom's shoulder didn't totally convince me it was real — I still had a sense of watching a drama unfold on TV rather than real life, and said as much to Tom.

"Oh, he's dead all right, and good riddance," he said.

I couldn't help but shudder at the thought that although he didn't know it, he was talking about his father.

It was some time later when I got to read the paper. Tom was busy in the garden and there was a knock on the front door. I opened it expecting to find John or Jess, but instead was surprised to see two strangers who introduced themselves as a Detective Inspector Bob Atkins and Detective Constable Steve Gaffney. My stomach did somersaults for no good reason, and I had an inexplicable feeling of guilt; but when they said it was Tom they had come to see, I was filled with dread. Then I remembered that Tom had left the village before 9am the day before and felt able to breathe again. Happy to let him do his own talking, I went to the back door and gave him a call. Both he and Fern came in together and Fern felt it incumbent upon her to give a token bark before rushing across to greet the visitors. I called her away and offered the detectives coffee, which they accepted, but as I made my way to the kitchen with Fern at my side, I heard DI Atkins ask Tom almost casually about his movements the previous day.

With the noise from the kettle boiling, I didn't hear anything else, but by the time I returned with the coffee the whole atmosphere had changed. The DC had risen to his feet and was now standing next to Tom's chair and DI Atkins was leaning forward in his chair, looking directly at Tom, who, although looking worried, also wore the stubborn look that I knew so well when he clammed up and refused to discuss something.

"So why did you go to his house?" said DI Atkins.

After a long pause, Tom almost whispered, "To talk about money."

I felt as if I had been kicked. Something was wrong. Tom couldn't have gone to Richard's house — he wouldn't have had time before catching the train.

"So you were short of money," said DC Gaffney. "Did he refuse to give you any and did you decide to help yourself?"

I felt the blood rush to my head and all my defences were on alert. "What the hell are you talking about?" I blurted out with a degree of anger I didn't recognise. "Tom caught a train at 9am and spent the day in Essex with friends, so how could he have helped himself to anything?"

"Please, Mrs Wilson, we are talking to Tom and he must answer for himself," said the Inspector.

"I didn't take anything. He made me so angry with his dirty remarks that I just walked out and didn't intend ever going back!" said Tom.

"So you were angry," said the constable. "Angry enough to want him dead, perhaps?"

"No!" said Tom. "I just walked out."

"We will need to take your fingerprints," said DI Atkins. "Perhaps you would like to come down to the station. Your Mum can come with you if you like, but we won't be questioning you any further at this time, and after we take your fingerprints you will be free to return home."

Tom looked stunned, but told me that he didn't want me to go with him, and then he walked out of the cottage with the two policemen like a condemned man. I sat down at the kitchen table in a state of shock, not knowing what to think. Why would he lie, and if he didn't go to Essex, where had he gone, as he didn't get home until long after me?

I was finding it hard to breathe and gripped onto the table as dizziness overtook me, and then I realised I was hyperventilating and becoming light-headed. I made a concerted effort to calm down, but I didn't know what to believe. I knew in my heart that Tom couldn't and wouldn't kill anyone; but, try as I might, I couldn't imagine why he'd lied to me about his plans for the day. The same question kept going around in my head: if he wasn't on the train, where the hell had he been all day? I didn't know what to do for the best, and wished I had insisted on going with him, but almost instinctively I picked up the phone and called John. I needed his support, and even with all my worry, I realised that for the first time in my life I had someone to share the bad times as well as the good.

When John arrived, he told me not to worry; he knew from his Dad that they followed every lead, however slight, and he was sure Tom wouldn't be the only one they had been talking to or taking fingerprints from. The whole thing seemed a waste of time to me, as Tom's fingerprints were bound to be in the house, as he often needed to go there to talk to Richard about the garden, and even more often when Richard wasn't there to talk to Beverley. However, John explained that this was probably just for elimination, as they needed to know which fingerprints should be there to exclude them from those that shouldn't. He felt the police were clutching at straws in the face of little firm evidence and, as yet, not even a definite cause of death, although he said that everyone seemed to know that it was the loss of blood from some sort of wound, which varied depending on who you listened to, from a slit throat to a stabbing.

We were still deep in conversation when Tom arrived home. It didn't seem five minutes since he'd left, and yet a glance at the clock showed he'd been gone just over an hour. Although obviously shaken by his ordeal, he didn't seem worried, and said that the police were happy with his explanation. I couldn't help the anger rising that was bubbling up inside me, and without stopping to think, I blurted out, "Well, the police might be happy with your explanation, but I'm not; perhaps you'd be good enough to tell me where you were yesterday!"

John, not wanting to become involved, made his excuses and left us to the argument that seemed inevitable, but my feelings of rage were all-consuming, and I hardly noticed him leave.

Unable to avoid the inquisition, Tom told me the same as he told the police: he'd wanted to ask Richard for a pay rise, and so decided to go and see him when no-one else was around, mostly to avoid the embarrassment of being turned down in front of Beverley. He'd taken a later train to Essex, but said he was so fed up and disappointed with Richard's response that he didn't want to talk about it.

"I thought if he'd just pay me a few extra quid I could save up for a car, and I really thought he might, because I'd worked so hard that he'd even noticed the garden was looking better. I should have known that there was no chance and not wasted my time, but now it seems I won't even have a job, let alone a pay rise!"

I really felt sorry for him now, but still felt obliged to remind him that he'd lied to me. As was his habit when found to be in the wrong, Tom became morose and uncommunicative to avoid further questioning, and I knew him well enough to know there was nothing more to be gleaned from this conversation; so, making it clear that I was hurt and disappointed by his behaviour, I brought the matter to a close. Although I couldn't put my finger on it, I had an uneasy feeling that there was more to all this than he was telling me, but there was no way he was willingly going to say any more at the moment, so I decided to bide my time.

The rest of Sunday passed uneventfully, and before long days drifted into weeks and the police presence left the village. There were still tatty faded posters on trees and noticeboards asking for information, but other than an occasional circuit by a squad car, very little seemed to be happening. Tom heard no more from the police and assumed they were satisfied with his explanation, and even Jess had heard very little, and didn't know when she would be able to arrange a funeral or sort out the house.

Then, suddenly, all thoughts of Richard were banished by some news from Jess. When she arrived at the cottage, beaming from ear to ear in the middle of the afternoon I was at first puzzled and then delighted to hear that she was three months pregnant. I hadn't known they were even trying for a baby and wondered if the pregnancy was planned, or if she was as surprised as I was; but one look at her face left me in no doubt she was delighted with her news, so I rushed forward to hug her.

"I'm so pleased for you; it's so exciting. Is Colin pleased? When are you due?"

All came out in a rush, and the next couple of hours were spent drinking tea at the kitchen table and discussing everything from names to natural childbirth and nursery decorations, and for the first time in a long while no image of Richard threw a cloud over the horizon. Jess was full of questions about Tom's birth, and I sensed some apprehension, but was able to tell her truthfully that from what I could remember there had been no complications and everything had gone very smoothly. I did point out that it was almost eighteen years ago and it was all a bit hazy. I asked her again what Colin thought about the news, and she suddenly realised that she'd come straight from the doctor and so hadn't yet told him! However, he did know she was going and why, and she realised he must be on tenterhooks waiting for the news. He was delighted with the prospect of becoming a father, but wouldn't start celebrating until he had confirmation. Jess asked to borrow the phone to call his office and I decided to go into the garden with Fern while Jess made her call, as I felt this was definitely a time for privacy. By the time I went back in, I met Jess coming out to meet me almost bursting with pride.

"He's very pleased," she said, but I knew from her face that this was an enormous understatement!

When she'd left, I once again had an uneasy feeling of envy. I was ashamed to realise that I had felt something similar when she'd planned her holiday, and now here it was again, the feeling that I was missing something. Almost as soon as the thought entered my head, I knew I was being silly — I had Tom and no need of other children. Nevertheless, talking to Jess had brought back all the memories of Tom as a baby, and my pride and fierce love for him when he was born, and there was a stirring of long-forgotten maternal instincts leaving me feeling distinctly broody. Almost immediately, John came into my mind and I laughed to myself when I imagined John's reaction to these feelings and realised, I must get a grip on myself or risk frightening him away. However, once the thought had entered my mind, I couldn't help wondering if he would ever want children, and if so, would he really want me?

The answer to that question came sooner than expected, for when John came over that evening and I told him Jess's news, his reaction wasn't what I expected.

"Lucky pair," he said. "They must be so happy, although it's a tremendous responsibility and must be quite a worry."

I was amazed by his maturity and took the chance to ask him if he wanted children, although I wasn't sure I wanted to hear his answer. It seemed ages before it came and it was obvious that he was giving the matter a great deal of thought.

"I don't know," he said. "Sometimes I think it would be great; but, as I said, it is a tremendous responsibility and I am not sure if I want to make that sort of commitment. Perhaps when the time is right; and anyway, it's not just down to me. How do you feel about it?"

I was stunned; this was the most positive indication that John saw us as a permanent couple and it took me completely by surprise.

Although he'd made comments about being together in the future, I had never dared believe in a conventional relationship; but this reference to my part in his family planning left me in no doubt that in his mind our future was together. It took me nearly as long to answer his question as he had taken over mine, and when I did speak, I still wasn't totally clear on what I was going to say. "I don't know if I will ever want another child, although I must admit I was a bit envious of Jess. Part of me is very broody, but then there is a selfish part that feels that I lost out on part of my childhood bringing up Tom and now I am ready to be free, although it makes me feel very guilty."

John said he understood and was quite relieved that I didn't want to start producing children, and although he didn't rule out the possibility in the future, he felt that at the moment he was happy to just enjoy me on my own. Although that brought the family planning to a close, we both knew that the conversation had changed our relationship, and it now seemed that we would stay together despite our age difference, our troubled beginnings and my troubled past — we were meant to be together, with or without children.

As the weeks turned into months and Jess grew bigger, Richard's sudden demise faded into the background. However, there was a sharp reminder when the police contacted Jess and gave her permission to arrange the funeral. It seemed pathology had found shards of glass from the broken French window in Richard's wounds, and in the light of this, the police had concluded that his death had been accidental. With no further evidence, that was the verdict reached at the Inquest, and although many questions were left unanswered, with no more information the police had nowhere to go, and it seemed that the only thing left to do was arrange the funeral, sell the house and bring the whole sorry mess to a close. Jess confessed to me that she didn't much fancy dealing with the formalities, especially in view of her size and imminent confinement, so I offered to help, although I had no idea what that involved. Jess and Colin had agreed to sell the house — neither of them fancied moving in, and with Colin's experience, they were assured of a good sale. As his only known relative, everything would come to Jess, but she told me that she was determined to do something for Tom, although neither of us could think how best to do it without it seeming odd. The will wouldn't be read until after the funeral, and other than details of Richard's wishes regarding his funeral, the solicitor who held the will had given no clues as to what it held, although there was no reason to expect any surprises.

Jess stuck religiously to Richard's wishes with regard to both the service and subsequent cremation at the crematorium in town and, at his request, there were no flowers and no hymns. The proceedings were sombre to the point of dull, and other than Jess and Colin, the only mourners were Tom and Beverley and me, more in an effort to support Jess than out of any respect for the deceased. I found it strange that Richard appeared to have no other friends or business associates to pay their last respects, and then I noticed DI Atkins hovering in the distance, and realised that despite the accidental death verdict, no-one really believed it, and anyone who knew Richard was probably still under suspicion.

After the funeral, the small gathering minus DI Atkins went back to Jess and Colin's house, where we were joined by prior arrangement by Richard's solicitor, Mr Adamson, who seemed eager to get on with his business and be on his way. As we thought, there were no surprises in Richard's will, and as Jess expected, everything came to her, other than one or two small bequests to distant relatives. The house and contents were worth a tidy sum and, together with Richard's various investments and business interests, would bring Jess considerable wealth. She told me afterwards that her instinct was to give it all away to charity, but, as I pointed out, some of the accumulated wealth had been her mother's, and anything from Richard was her right, and in some respects her compensation. Jess replied that the same could be said of me and she was determined to do something for both Tom and me, but wasn't sure what.

Chapter 12
A NEW LIFE

Tom's college course didn't start until April, but as we were well into March there seemed little chance of him getting any work before then. Although he still saw Beverley regularly, neither of them had any spare cash to go out, as she, too, was still job hunting, and as the evenings pulled in, they couldn't even go out for walks. Tom spent more and more time with Jack Butler, helping him in his garden as his illness began to take its toll. Although he could no longer work in the garden he loved, Jack still had a lot to offer in the way of knowledge, and took great pleasure from teaching Tom to keep it just as he liked it. They spent hours talking about all things horticultural, and Beverley often joined them in the evenings, and they would sit by the fire and chat. The conversation was mostly about themselves and what they were doing, which Jack loved to hear, but sometimes it was Jack's own memories they listened to, and they were both fascinated to hear these, and used to come home and share them with me.

Jack talked mostly about his life since he moved to the village about thirty years before, and he told them about village life, the children he'd taught and the pranks they got up to. Some of them still lived in the village, including Beverley's father, and Jack could remember Beverley's mother and talked fondly of her as a small child. He often reminded Beverley about her own days in his classroom, which always made Tom laugh, and they were both amazed at how accurate his memories were of all the children that he'd taught, even though most had left the village many years before. Jack never said much about his personal life, although they did discover he'd been married before he came to the village, but his wife had died. Although he never elaborated on the circumstances of her death, his obvious distress when he talked about her led them to believe it was a tragic loss, and discouraged them from asking questions.

I was happy that they had befriended Jack, for he hardly ever came to the shop since his illness had progressed, and I had been afraid that he was spending all his time alone. I made a point of calling in to see him when I had an hour or two to spare, at first out of kindness, but as time went on, I found I really looked forward to my visits and went as much for myself as for him. Jack had a wisdom and understanding probably acquired from so many years working with children, and I found I could talk to him about anything and everything. It was to Jack that I first confessed my feelings for John, and was relieved by his total acceptance and genuine delight in my happiness. It was Jack who listened to my worries about Tom and put them into perspective, assuring me that he would turn out fine and make me proud, and it was Jack who was the only one, other than Jess, who had worked out who I really was, and surprised me by revealing that he'd known all along. This all came about when I was listening to him reminiscing about his time at the school and suddenly recalling an incident. "Do you remember when you and Jess were late because you had taken that stray dog home on the way to school and you arrived covered in muddy paw prints?" he laughed.

I was astounded and didn't know what to say; it all sounded so natural, as if Jack had been recalling memories of me every time he saw me, and yet he'd never given me away or even hinted that he knew who I was. I briefly considered denial, but one look at Jack's dear face convinced me that this would be useless, and anyway he deserved better, so I simply said, "How long have you known?"

"Oh, my dear, I knew you as soon as I saw you, but I realised you didn't want to be recognised, so I didn't see any reason to spoil things for you. I don't know why you went away; I only know that you were one of my favourite pupils, and I was so sorry to see you leave. To have you back in the village with the added bonus of your lovely son is a pleasure I never expected. I wouldn't want to say anything that would spoil it and drive you away again, so I've been very careful, but I may not be around much longer and I can't bear the thought of leaving you without telling you how fond I am of you and how much I missed you when you went away so suddenly."

I was surprised but also touched by the obvious depth of Jack's feeling for me, but was at a loss as to why this should be. I remembered that he was always very kind to me when I was at school, but I couldn't imagine why he remained so fond after all these years. I didn't feel any threat or hint of a hidden agenda, and I realised that his feelings for me were pure, kind, and almost paternal, so although unexpected, and very possibly undeserved, they were nevertheless very welcome. With this new closeness I felt drawn to Jack and spent nearly as much time at his cottage as Tom and Beverley, enjoying long chats and discovering a shared humour that gave us both a great deal of pleasure.

Tom had told me how entertaining and interesting he found Jack in spite of him being so ill, and I was finding out how true this was. I was so glad that Tom had found such an honourable male role model in the absence of a father, but was concerned about how he, and indeed I, would deal with Jack's inevitable fate, knowing how losing his grandmother had put Tom's life into a downward spiral. However, I thought this was unlikely now he was older, and he'd certainly grown up a great deal since we moved to the village. He'd also developed ambition and a clear direction, but most of all he'd found Beverley, and I realised that this had made a man of him. I realised that I, too, had found John, and somehow, we would all do whatever we could for Jack while he was with us and would miss him terribly when he was gone, but I realised with sudden conviction that we would cope.

It wasn't long before I heard from Jess that after several meetings with the solicitors and all the paperwork completed, she was finally able to put Richard's house on the market, and with his connections in the property market Colin was able to send several prospective buyers to view. In what seemed a very short space of time, it was sold to a couple from London who worked in the city but wanted a "country bolthole" to retreat to at weekends. Jess told me that the wife was a solicitor and the husband a QC, so there seemed no lack of funds, and the sale went through without a hitch.

As soon as the sale was completed, and Jess was in possession of the funds, she once again raised the subject of doing something for Tom and me. Even though I tried my best to convince her there was no need, she was insistent, but had absolutely no idea how or what she should do. In the event, the whole problem went out of her mind with the onset of labour, and when her waters broke suddenly and unceremoniously on her kitchen floor while she was arguing the point with me, she accepted that the time wasn't right and was quite happy to summon Colin and head for the hospital.

I couldn't help worrying about her, even though I knew there was really no need. She was a strong, healthy woman and childbirth was a perfectly natural event. However, I allowed myself to contemplate a pessimistic outlook, and this brought home to me how close we had become. I was also slightly worried how much this baby might change our relationship, and was still in this frame of mind when the telephone rang and a delighted Colin announced the birth of Paul Adam. He told me that Jess was asking to see me and couldn't wait to show him to me, so I realised that all my worries had been for nothing, and I rushed off to get a card as well as flowers, wine and toys to congratulate Jess and Colin and welcome Paul Adam.

As I gazed at the tiny bundle in the cot beside Jess, my heart went out to this perfect little stranger, just as it had all those years ago with Tom. He thankfully bore no resemblance to his grandfather, but had a familiar look to him, which I realised wasn't anything to do with Jess or her father. Paul Adam, even at this tender age, was a carbon copy of his own father, which I mentioned to Jess, much to her delight.

When given the opportunity to pick Paul up for a cuddle, I was surprised at how comfortable I was, as all my maternal instincts came flooding back, and it was as if I was once again holding Tom. I think Jess sensed this and knew that, like a guardian angel, I would always be here for him, and she chose that moment to ask me to be his Godmother.

Jess brought Paul home the following day and slipped naturally into her new role, so life soon returned to normal. I was so pleased that she visited just as often, but now there were two of them, and I couldn't help but be impressed with how well she coped, remembering my own inept efforts with Tom in the first few days of his life. Paul was a naturally happy and contented baby, and watching her tenderness with her son brought back vivid memories of her mother, and the resemblance was almost uncanny. It seemed obvious that Richard's influence hadn't infiltrated either the physical resemblance or characteristics of his daughter, although he'd doubtless played havoc with her mind.

As Paul began to grow and develop his own character, he became more and more entertaining. When they came to visit me or I went to Jess's house, we spent many happy hours just watching Paul at play, and delighting in the company of this little person whose face broke into a huge grin at the sight of me. I was often trusted to babysit when Jess met with solicitors and insurance agents in an effort to sort out Richard's complicated estate, and on these occasions, I was pleased to find that I could slip into the role of substitute Mummy quite easily. One real bonus was the strong bond that developed between Paul and Fern. From the moment that the baby was first brought into the cottage, tucked up asleep in his carrycot, Fern was fascinated. From an initial curiosity, she developed her own maternal instincts and whenever Paul was around, Fern was stationed close by. Fern took her job as self-appointed guardian very seriously, and decided early on that Rosie and Daisy were not allowed near the baby. Jess and I ached from holding in our laughter as Fern gently but firmly ushered the cats out every time they dared to show their faces when Paul was about, and the perplexed look on the cats' faces was a picture, as they were pushed out of the back door by Fern.

No sooner had things settled down after the new arrival than, like a dog with a bone, Jess was once again back on the subject of helping Tom. She realised I was worried about arousing his suspicions, but thought we could get round the problem by inventing a long-lost dead relative, and I began to warm to the idea. Before long we were like a couple of conspirators planning how to dispose of Richard's vast accumulated wealth, which neither of us wanted. Eventually, we decided to set aside enough to give Tom a bit of a start in life and then give the rest to charity. We decided caring for abused children was the best use of the money, so decided to find a charity that did just that, and make the gift anonymous so that no glory would be attached to the name of a man who so little deserved it. Once the decision was made, Jess set about finding the right charity while I applied myself once again to deception. It was a shame that once again I would lie to my son, but knowing that it was for his own good and would save him pain helped. I decided to give my grandmother a long-lost brother who knew all about Tom from letters that she'd written, and had taken quite a lot of interest in this great-nephew. I persuaded Jess to make the bequest a modest one and so hopefully more believable, and we decided to tell him about it that evening.

I waited until we had finished tea before launching into my well-rehearsed story about the great-uncle who knew all about him. However, nothing I said in any way prepared him for the news, as although he'd been half-listening, he really wasn't taking much notice, and he was completely bowled over when I told him about the £10,000 bequest. He was convinced it was a wind-up and refused to be taken in, but when I managed to convince him it was real, his smile said it all.

"I'm almost sorry he's dead," he said. "He must have been a really nice bloke; but then if he wasn't dead, I wouldn't have his money, so I can't be too sad!"

I could see the sense in this and smiled to myself at the resilience of youth.

"I think he was very old," I said in an effort to justify our obvious delight in his death, and then remembered that he didn't actually exist, which in itself was pretty funny. Tom was already making plans, for suddenly all things were possible and, not surprisingly, his first thoughts were for Beverley.

"I must tell Beverley! We can have a car and I can take her out; she'll be so excited," he said.

But when he rushed off to see her, I had a feeling that he'd bigger plans than he was willing to share.

Thoughts of Tom and his future were banished from my mind when John turned up. Despite all the time spent with Jess and Paul and the planning required to set up Tom's legacy, John was never far from my thoughts, and we spent most evenings and weekends together.

The village and even John's parents seemed to have accepted us as a couple, despite his mother's original misgivings. It was easier for Roger, his father, as he'd known me from the early training days and saw me as more than just the "older woman"; but for Jackie, his Mum, it had been much more difficult. However, as the months went by and I occasionally helped out at the kennels working alongside John at busy times, Jackie had seen how well we worked together and seemed to soften. We developed what started as a mutual respect, which had recently warmed to friendship. She had the same sense of humour as her son, and he was so much like her in many ways it was easy for me to like her, and our relationship became so much easier once we began to laugh together.

When John arrived on this particular evening he was almost bursting with news, but told me to get dressed up as he was taking me for a meal which was already booked, as he'd something he needed to tell me. Intrigued, but unable to get any more information, I went upstairs to change. Knowing Tom was out for the evening, John followed me upstairs and told me that there was plenty of time, as the meal wasn't booked until eight and it was only just six. Although I stood with my back to John, his close proximity and obvious excitement caused my heart to beat faster as I felt the now familiar desire well up inside me. Reading my thoughts, John put his hands on my shoulders and turned me round to face him. With slow, tender movements, he helped me out of my clothes and led me to the bed, and as we kissed, we lost sight of everything except our need for each other. Since our first tentative beginnings, our lovemaking had become totally fulfilling, and John's heady mixture of sensualistic tenderness and unrestrained passion brought me to heights of pleasurable climax, synchronised with his own — together we could fly!

Completely satisfied, we lay for some time in each other's arms without a word being spoken, totally in harmony with each other and unwilling to shatter the perfection of the moment. Eventually, John reminded me about our dinner engagement, and we dragged ourselves back to the real world with some reluctance.

Just over an hour later, we entered the lounge of the Swan Hotel, where our meal was booked. Curious about the motive behind this particular date and taking my cue from John, who had arrived looking immaculate in a suit, I had made a special effort and felt quite glamorous in my one and only "little black dress". Looking around at the rather grand surroundings, I was pleased with my choice, and didn't feel out of place in the rather sumptuous restaurant. I had only ever passed this place a few times, and never before been inside, but it harked back to a time when fine dining was the norm and people dressed for dinner. When the waiter came to show us to our candle-lit table, I felt like I was in a Hollywood movie, and I was so proud to have this handsome co-star at my side. Still basking in the afterglow of our lovemaking, our conversation was easy and relaxed through the first two courses, and, unused to wine, I was enjoying the slight feeling of intoxication and the warm glow of well-being that the accompanying Chardonnay induced. It came as a complete surprise, therefore, when the conversation took on a more serious note as we perused the dessert menu. At first, I wasn't really listening as I debated between Peach Melba and Chocolate Gateau, but I suddenly took notice when I heard, "We can take over the kennels! I've spoken to them and they know how things are between us, so are happy to leave the kennels in our hands once we are married."

I was speechless. The prospect of running the kennels was tremendously exciting, but that paled into insignificance in the light of John's reference to marriage.

Seeing my stunned expression, John took it for reluctance, and in an incredulous voice said, "Don't you want to marry me?"

I found my voice and, even in such extreme circumstances, saw the humour of the situation. "It would be nice to be asked," I said.

John was immediately contrite and took my hand across the table. "Do you want me to go down on my knees?" he said, but, terrified that he might actually do so, I assured him that I was happy with him sitting down.

"Rachel, my lovely, smiling, beautiful Rachel, will you marry me?" he said, and, without a moment's hesitation, I heard myself say "Yes."

The rest of the evening passed in a blur, and although we did make plans and talk of the future, it seemed like it was all happening around me while I basked in the glow of loving and being loved.

Later, when I finally settled down to bed that night, it occurred to me that I was going to spend the rest of my life with the man that gave that life back to me, and this brought me a feeling of contentment deep inside which I had never known before. It was hard to believe how much had happened in just one day, but, thinking back, I realised that this is the way life had been ever since I'd heard about the cottage in the crusty old solicitor's office. It was incredible to think that in little more than two years my life had taken such a dramatic turn, and here I was on the brink of marriage to someone whose love had changed my life and restored my faith in men. There seemed little doubt now that Tom and Beverley had a future together, and the special love that I had developed for Jack over the past few months made him feel like the loving father I had never had. Jess was more like a sister than a friend, and Colin and little Paul made the family complete. For the first time in my life, I felt as if I was part of a loving family and I really had come home.

Chapter 13
CONCLUSION

Jack knew that his life was ending. He felt neither fear nor sadness, just a firm conviction that he would soon be with his beloved Ellen. As he drifted in and out of consciousness, he was sometimes aware of familiar voices around him. He was touched that Tom and Beverley sat for endless hours at his bedside, chatting away to him even though, as the drugs took away his pain, he found himself less and less able to respond. He was aware that Rachel often came to see him, and his one regret was that he couldn't talk to her and tell her all the things he'd kept bottled up inside for so long. However, all this paled into insignificance as his befuddled mind rolled back the years, and he was once again a handsome young man hand in hand with his beautiful bride as they walked into the sunshine to begin their married life.

The pictures in his head were much clearer than the vague shapes that surrounded his bed, and so he sought refuge in his memories and allowed his mind to transport him back. It seemed to Jack that he'd always loved Ellen. Growing up in a small village, they had known each other all their lives, gone to the same school, and continued to meet after school when Jack left a couple of years earlier than Ellen. Neither of them could imagine life without the other, and they just accepted that they would spend their lives together. Even their ambitions matched, and they both hoped to teach and talked of training and working together, perhaps even taking on their own village school or going abroad to teach together. When Ellen eventually left school, too, they were ready to put their plans into action, but European rumblings put an end to any thoughts of travelling, and Jack was soon called away to serve his country. Their lives were on hold for six long years, but with infrequent letters and even rarer home leave, they managed to keep in touch. Jack's memories of the war were not pleasant, but he remembered feeling lucky to be alive, and knowing Ellen was waiting gave him the strength to endure the bloody battlefield and retain his sanity.

When the hostilities finally ceased, Jack returned an older and wiser man who, although physically unscathed, still suffered a certain amount of mental anguish over the sights seen and the friends lost. Ellen was the salve that healed his psychological wounds, and within months of his return they were walking out of the village chapel as husband and wife, determined to fulfil all their early plans. While Jack had been away, Ellen had completed her teacher training and was able to support Jack while he, too, trained and qualified to teach. It seemed as if nothing could stop their dreams from coming true, and when they applied for and were accepted as teachers in charge of the school in the next village with its own school house, their lives were complete, or so they thought, until Ellen discovered she was pregnant. Jack remembered how they had hugged and danced and hugged some more when Ellen told him the news, and the months that followed went by in a blur of painting and knitting and planning for the arrival of this very welcome addition to their family.

Jack suddenly became aware of his surroundings once again as the District Nurse leaned over to administer more morphine. He didn't know if it was the pain of the present or the pain of the past that had brought him back, but he knew that Rachel was sitting by his bed and felt strangely comforted knowing that she was there. As the morphine took effect, he felt himself drifting back, but was reluctant to return to the part of his life that had brought him such sorrow. Death has no respect for feelings, and reluctantly Jack faced the part of his life that still caused him so much distress. When the time came for Ellen to go into the little country hospital, neither of them were worried. Ellen had sailed through her pregnancy with barely a hint of sickness and she looked and felt well even after her pains began. However, as her labour progressed, Jack, waiting outside, sensed that things were not going well. Nurses rushed in and out of the room and more than one doctor was summoned. Jack was virtually ignored and wasn't told anything, except not to worry, which was, in fact, more worrying, and when after a day and a half Ellen still continued to labour without issue, Jack was distraught. Feeling frustrated and helpless, he finally managed to collar a doctor, who told him there were complications and they were in danger of losing the baby. Jack was devastated, but his first thoughts were for Ellen and he pleaded to be allowed to see her. The doctor told him that the birth was imminent but, as they were expecting a stillbirth, he would be needed to comfort Ellen when it was all over. Jack remembered the surprise and elation he felt when, against all odds, he heard the first cry of his child, and when he was finally allowed to see them both he knew he would never forget Ellen's face as she cuddled her baby daughter, almost bursting with happiness and pride.

Even in his unconscious state, Jack remembered the acute joy followed by the intense pain he felt when Ellen's condition deteriorated and, just three day later, he lost her. He was inconsolable and handled his grief with anger. He demanded to know what had gone wrong and blamed the doctors, the nurses and even himself; but, most of all, he blamed the baby. He refused to see her or take responsibility for her, and without any hesitation, he signed the papers that freed her up for adoption. He walked away from the hospital, leaving his baby without a backward glance, much to the dismay of family and friends, and once Ellen's funeral was over he gave up his job and moved away and lost himself in a downward spiral of grief and alcohol.

He finally came to his senses when an unexpected visit from Ellen's mother forced him to see what he'd become, living off unemployment benefit in a scruffy bed-sit. When she found him surrounded by empty bottles, she had no hesitation in telling him what she thought of him and how disappointed Ellen would have been to see his sorry state, and her words filled him with shame. So when she went on to tell him the reason for her visit, he was ready to listen. It seemed that ever since Jack had walked away and left his baby, Grace had followed her progress. By devious means, she'd discovered who had adopted her, and where she was living, and had determined to keep an eye on her until she was grown up, just in case the child should need her. Sadly, she'd recently found out that she didn't have long to live, and with her husband already dead there was no one to watch over her grand-daughter and make sure she was never alone. Her unselfish love for a baby that she'd never even held both overwhelmed and shamed Jack, and he was keenly aware of denying her the chance of bringing up her daughter's baby by his own selfish act. Grace had spent weeks looking for Jack ever since she'd been given her devastating diagnosis, and instead of feeling sorry for herself, all her thoughts were for her grand-daughter. Once she'd found Jack, she decided to ask him to take on the responsibility of unofficial guardian angel; but now, seeing his pitiful state, she was doubtful about the wisdom of this plan. However, she had little or no choice, and there was enough of her daughter about her to have a profound effect on her son-in-law. Jack knew he must pull himself together — he owed it to this woman who had taken on his responsibility, and he promised her he would get his life straightened out and carry out her wishes.

This was the turning point, and within a relatively short time Jack had cleaned up his act and was ready to start teaching again. Grace had given him all the details she knew about his daughter, so when the job came up in the small village where she was growing up he knew it was meant to be. That was how he came to the village, and before long came face to face with Rachel, the daughter on whom he'd turned his back before ever meeting her. Although he'd taken on the role of guardian angel somewhat reluctantly out of duty, as soon as he set eyes on the miniature version of his lovely Ellen he knew that he could never walk away again. With Rachel attending the small village school and under his tutelage, it was hard for Jack not to show favouritism, but there was never a need for discipline with this happy and friendly child who was an avid learner and a kind and sensitive friend. Jack watched with pride as her friendship developed with Jess and her fierce protection of her friend after her mother died was touching. So much of what Jack saw was reminiscent of Ellen that it was impossible for him not to love her, and he was so sad that he could never tell her how much. He knew he'd only himself to blame, but dreamed that one day it would be possible to tell her the truth and try to make her understand.

Jack returned from his dreaming to the reality of his impending demise and realised that the sun was no longer streaming through his bedroom window. In a rare lucid moment, his saw the outline of Rachel's face and tried to reach out his hand to her, and she almost instinctively moved forward to take his hand in hers. Once again Jack regretted his inability to communicate, but consoled himself with the knowledge that every detail of his life was meticulously recorded in a series of diaries which Rachel would receive after his death. He was saddened that he wouldn't be there to help her understand, and fearful that she would end up hating him, but he knew that she deserved the truth and was confident that she had the strength to cope with it.

Thinking of Rachel's strength took him back to the day that she disappeared from the village and the reason for it, although at the time Jack couldn't find out what had happened to her. By this time she'd moved up to the senior school in town and he saw much less of her. He knew she stayed friends with Jess and spent a lot of time with her, and Jack remembered feeling somewhat complacent about his role at that time, as Rachel had shown all the hoped-for promise academically, and was a well-adjusted, happy girl. She was bright enough to go on to university and he'd felt sure that her life was on track and she would always do well. Then, suddenly, she disappeared! He desperately tried to find out where she was, but all he could discover was that she was living with her grandmother and wouldn't be returning to the village. There was no explanation, and it was difficult for him to ask too many questions without appearing somewhat suspicious. He hoped to find out something from Jess, but when he did meet her briefly she just repeated the same story and didn't even seem to know where this grandmother lived. Jack racked his brains to think of a way of discovering what had happened, and the answer came when he received details of a writing competition, which he was sure Rachel would want to enter. He decided to visit her adoptive parents, in the hope that this would give him a valid reason to find out where she was. He had a spring in his step as he walked to the cottage, but was both surprised and shocked by the hostility he encountered when he got there. They told him she'd gone away and wouldn't be coming back, and when he asked if he could forward the details of the competition to her, they said she would have no time for such things and refused to give him her address.

When Rachel disappeared from his life for the second time it was very hard, and it felt almost like losing Ellen all over again. He blamed himself for not being able to find her, and believed that he'd let both Grace and Ellen down by failing to watch over her. As the years went by, Jack immersed himself in his work and took pleasure in the successes of his pupils. He never forgot Rachel, but just learned to live with his loss, as he'd done with her mother. Sometimes he feared he'd forgotten them both, and struggled to recall their faces, but when Rachel walked back into his life as a grown woman and the replica of her mother, he knew he hadn't forgotten. If Rachel remembered him she gave no sign, and it was apparent that she didn't want people to remember her. He was puzzled by this, and by her change of name, and when he discovered she had a grown-up son he started to do some arithmetic. Suddenly it all fell into place and Jack knew the reason for her hasty departure. He was saddened that she'd had to grow up so suddenly, and couldn't think how it had happened, as to his knowledge she had never had a boyfriend, and had shown no interest in finding one, spending all her time with Jess. There were no clues when he met Tom, as he looked exactly like Jack's own father, and despite the circumstances of his birth, he warmed to this unknown grandson. As he got to know him better, he found he'd inherited his own love of the garden, and they immediately struck up a friendship which became a very important part of both of their lives.

Jack went out of his way to get to know Rachel again, and sometimes thought she knew that he recognised her. He made a point of calling in with fresh vegetables and flowers and often spent time in the garden with Tom, and so regularly sat drinking tea in the cottage with a cat on his lap and Fern at his feet. It was on one of these visits that his curiosity was satisfied, although at the time he wished it hadn't been. Tom had told him about the greenfly problem he was having in the garden and Jack decided to go round and spray the roses for him. He knew that Tom would be at work and thought Rachel was out, too, so he let himself into the back garden and set to work. After a short while, Fern joined him in the garden and he realised that Rachel must have come home, but as he walked to the back door to say hello he saw Jess sitting at the kitchen table and decided not to interrupt. He was just turning to go back to his work when he realised that both Jess and Rachel seemed upset and he found himself standing by the open back door, listening to their conversation. Afterwards, he felt ashamed at eavesdropping, but at the time he couldn't drag himself away as the awful truth of what he was hearing sank in. After a while, consumed with rage, he knew he must leave, for if Rachel knew he'd overheard she would be devastated. Although he'd fought his way through a world war, he'd never before felt the desire to kill, but suddenly he wanted to put an end to the man who had defiled his daughter, and caused her so much suffering. He realised that he must go home and calm down, for he was in danger of doing something silly; but he was determined that Richard would know the extent of his evil and face the consequences, even though he'd no idea yet how to make this happen.

The anger he felt as he recalled this incident once again roused him back to consciousness, and his obvious distress brought Rachel to his side again. He'd lost all sense of time and didn't know if she'd been there for hours or days. Her care and compassion made him feel so well loved that, for a brief moment, he wanted to fight the inevitable and return to the living world and this beautiful daughter. His restlessness obviously upset Rachel and she called for the nurse to make him more comfortable. Soon his physical pain faded and he drifted back to the dream world where his life took place before him like a gripping drama.

After Jack had overheard the girls talking that day, he started to make his plan. He would confront Richard, tell him what he knew, and then threaten him with police involvement. He hoped this would drive Richard out of the country, as he had no wish to carry out his threat. Making Rachel, Tom and Jess's stories public knowledge would only hurt them all, but he believed he could scare Richard enough to make him leave and, in the circumstances, he thought this would be his best hope. He wasn't in any way violent, but he knew that he could lose his temper with this man, and although he was prepared to spend the rest of his own life in prison for the satisfaction of ending his, he knew that this would result in an enquiry that would open too many old wounds.

Jack was aware of Tom's relationship with Beverley and couldn't risk her being in the house when he confronted Richard in case she overheard anything, and so when Tom told him about them both having the day off on Richard's birthday, it seemed like a heaven-sent opportunity. When the Saturday arrived, Jack made his way to the big house. Although sure of his ground, he was feeling apprehensive as he approached the big front door, wondering how Richard would take what he had to say. He was just about to knock when he heard a scream from the back of the house. Although no longer able to run, he hurried as best he could round the side of the house and, as he reached the back, he saw Richard wrestling with a young girl in front of the French windows. As he moved closer, he recognised the girl as Lynda, Beverley's younger sister, and Richard's intentions towards her were obvious. He was still a good way away, but Jack yelled out to Richard to let her go. As Richard heard the shout, he was momentarily distracted, and Lynda gave him an almighty shove against the French windows. As Jack reached the window, he heard the glass shatter, and saw Lynda run past him without appearing even to notice him. Her hair was wild, her eyes were streaming, and she had a look of sheer terror on her face. Jack turned back to see Richard on the floor, half in and half out of the windows, which had burst open with the impact, and on closer inspection he could see the large shard of glass protruding from his neck. Richard gasped for help and tried to grab Jack's legs as he passed by him into the house, but Jack felt only contempt and made no effort to assist him.

Once inside the room, Jack sat calmly in the big leather chair, looking across at Richard, who had managed to drag himself back into the room. Without a hint of pity, despite Richard's pleadings, Jack began to speak. In a cold and clear voice, devoid of any emotion, he told Richard every detail of the sordid story that he'd discovered and, as he talked, he watched the colour drain from his face. Richard tried desperately to defend himself, babbling on about love and loneliness, but his shock was apparent when he discovered that Tom was his son, and with that, the realisation and fear of the consequences. Nevertheless, he still had an overwhelming instinct to survive, but knowing that there would be no help from this quarter, he desperately tried to pull himself towards the telephone on the small table next to Jack and breathed a sigh of relief when he saw Jack turn to pick it up. However, his relief turned to terror when, standing up slowly, Jack picked up the phone in one hand and the table in the other and moved both to the other side of the room. Turning back once more, he looked long and hard at Richard, who by now was drifting in and out of consciousness, and then without a word he turned away and walked out of the house.

Jack started to breathe more deeply now, and those around his bed knew he was nearing his end. As his breathing slowed and his body relaxed, a beautiful smile lit his face and he slipped peacefully away.

For Jack it seemed there wasn't anything left to do now Richard was gone. He knew that Rachel was happy with her John, and Tom would settle with Beverley, and what he wanted more than anything else in this world was to see Ellen in the next. He was afraid that his failure to help Richard might result in him losing the chance to see his beloved again, but as he closed his eyes, he heard her call to him and suddenly he was no longer in the darkened bedroom but in a beautiful place where Ellen stood, her arms outstretched to welcome him. Jack was at peace.